SOULS OF THE DEAD

ROBERT J. RANDISI

SOULS OF THE DEAD

Book 2 of the Hitman With A Soul Trilogy

Down & Out Books
3959 Van Dyke Rd, Ste. 265
Lutz, FL 33558
www.DownAndOutBooks.com

Cover art and design by JT. Lindroos
Cover photo by Glen Edelson

ISBN: 193749585X

ISBN-13: 978-1-937495-85-5

To Marthayn.
Not only my heart,
But my soul, as well.

*"Burn it, with the souls of the dead
Souls of the Dead
bring forth their reincarnation"*

— Souls of the Dead,
Kalodin

PROLOGUE
Monday night . . .

Ex-Sheriff Ken Burke entered Pirates alley from the Jackson Square end. All the businesses and activities that attracted tourists to the Square had closed by 8 p.m. Now, at 11 p.m., it was deserted, except for some homeless people looking to sleep on benches, or in doorways.

Burke walked along the side of the St. Louis Cathedral. His meet was set for behind the building, across from the Faulkner House.

The ex-Orleans Parish Sheriff moved as carefully and quietly as he could. In his belt he had his old .45. The gun had retired with him, never having given way to the S&W and Beretta double-action, semi-automatic pistols that were also eventually eclipsed by the appearance of the Glock. These were the guns law enforcement officials began to carry during what Burke referred to as the "new age" of law enforcement. He was still "old age" in his thinking, though he recognized the irony and didn't like the first impression the phrase presented.

But as alert as he was, the old reflexes were not what they used to be. He heard a sound behind him. Before he could turn toward it something struck him on the back of the head and he went down.

Goddamn, but getting old was a bitch!

ONE

When Sangster's phone rang it came as a surprise.

Not only because it was the middle of the night, but because Sangster's phone never rang. Not ever, except for an occasional wrong number. He only kept the land line because he didn't own a cell phone. When he had need of one, he always bought the disposable kind.

He groped in the dark for the receiver, wanting nothing more than for the ringing to stop.

"Yes, what?" he said.

"Mr. Stark?"

Richard Stark was a name he used when he didn't want to use Sangster.

"Who's calling?"

"Sir, this is the Urgent Care center in University Hospital? Are you Mr. Richard Stark?"

"That's right."

"You've been listed as the person to be notified—"

"What?" he asked, sitting up. "Listed by who? What are you talking about?"

"Um, a man named Kenneth Burke? He's been injured and gave your name and number—"

"Is he all right?" Sangster asked. "Is he alive?"

"He's alive, sir," the woman said, "but you'll need to come down—"

"I'll be there," Sangster said. "I'm—it'll take me a while—I'm coming from Algiers, but I'll be there as soon as I can."

"All right, sir."

"Take care of him," Sangster said, "take good care of

him. I'll pay, understand? Money's no object."

"We're taking care of him, sir," she said. "That's our job."

"Okay, okay." He almost hung up, then put the phone back to his ear. "Who are you? I mean, what's your name?"

"I'm Nurse Claire O'Malley, sir," she said. "I'll be on duty when you get here."

"Okay," he said, "I'll be there."

"Yes, all right, si—"

He hung up, got out of bed and grabbed some clothes. . .

Outside of Sangster's house the man called Quinlan was watching from across the street, trying to get the lay of the land. He had only arrived in New Orleans that afternoon, got himself situated in a small B&B before heading out to find Algiers Point. He got directions from the woman who ran the B&B, an attractive middle-aged brunette who was obviously flirting. Maybe, if he was there long enough, he could look into that.

Once he got directions to Algiers he grabbed a cab to the ferry and took the ride across. He used most of the rest of the day to check the area out, look for cops and, finally, locate Sangster's house.

He was there long enough for the last ferry to have left, so he decided to spend the night outside of Sangster's house. He wasn't ready to go in. He was good at his job, and that meant learning all he could about his target, and the target's environment.

That's why he was there when the front door opened and Sangster came rushing out. The man got into an old Ford and drove off fast. The ferry still wasn't running, but Quinlan had been told there was a bridge you could take back and forth. He didn't have a car, though, so there was no way to follow Sangster. But that was okay. He needed to learn the set-up of the house, anyway. And he could do that while Sangster was gone.

Upon arrival at University Hospital on Perdido Street, Sangster parked the car he'd borrowed from in front of Burke's house and sought out and found Nurse O'Malley, a pretty woman in her thirties with freckles and a mass of red curls that she'd tried to pin up under her nurse's cap.

"Oh, yes, Mr. Stark," she said. "Uh, your friend is still being treated. I'll take you to talk to the doctor."

"Thank you."

"The police are here, as well."

"The police?" Sangster asked. "Why?"

"Well, apparently your friend had been attacked," she said, "and he had some sort of badge on him?"

"He's a retired Sheriff," Sangster said.

"I see." She led Sangster deeper into the emergency room. Around him were people with all different sorts of injuries, a couple of which seemed to be pretty bloody.

"You're busy," he observed.

"Yes, sir," she said. "Since Katrina caused Charity Hospital to close down, we pick up a lot of extra cases. We pretty much split them with Tulane Hospital."

The ex-hitman followed the nurse, hoping the police officers wouldn't be too interested in who he was and he'd be able to get away with saying he was "a friend."

As it turned out, he needn't have worried. He saw two men talking to a tall, very skinny white-coated doctor, recognized them, immediately, and knew they would recognize him. The doctor was wearing a name tag that read, DR. JUDD, M.D.

"Doctor?" she said. "This is Mr. Burke's emergency contact."

The doctor and both detectives turned to face Sangster.

"Well, look who it is," Detective Williams said. "Stark, right?"

"Mr. Stark," Detective Aaron Telemaco said. "I should have realized—"

"How is Burke?" Sangster demanded.

The doctor looked at Telemaco for guidance, and the older detective nodded and said, "You can go ahead and answer, Doc."

"Mr. Burke was attacked on the street," the doctor said. His watery eyes studied Sangster from behind rimless wire-frame glasses. "He has a nasty lump on the back of his head, but no other obvious injuries."

"What do you mean, 'obvious injuries'?" Sangster asked.

"Well, just that," the doctor said. "He's in and out of consciousness."

"Is that unusual with a head injury?" Sangster asked.

"Well, no . . ."

"But?"

"But this seems odd," the doctor said. "I was just telling the detectives, we've taken x-rays and a cat scan, and we can't see any reason for his condition."

"He was hit on the head," Sangster said.

"As I said," the doctor went on, "he has a lump, but no concussion. He should be back on his feet by now."

"Well . . ." Sangster said. ". . . he is an older man."

"Even taking that into account," the doctor said, "he should be up."

"Have you tried to get him on his feet?"

"He can't stand," the man said. "He seems to be suffering from extreme vertigo."

"So what are you going to do?"

"We were waiting for you to arrive," the doctor said. "You're his emergency contact. Are you family?"

"Mr. Stark is Sheriff Burke's neighbor," Telemaco said, "and good friend."

"Then you'll have to make the decision as to how we proceed from here."

"What would you like to do?" Sangster asked.

"Well. . . I'd admit him so we can run some more tests," Doctor Judd said, "see if we can't track down just what the problem is."

"Then do that."

"Um," Dr. Judd said, "I assume Mr. Burke has Medicare? Or some kind of insurance?"

"I'll take care of that," Sangster said. "You just find what's wrong with him."

"Okay, then."

"Can I see him?"

"It'll be a while before we can move him into a room," Judd said. "The nurse will show you where he is."

That was the first time Sangster noticed that the nurse was still there.

"Hold on, Stark," Williams said, "we wanna talk—"

"Let Mr. Stark see the Sheriff, Ben," Telemaco said. "We can talk later."

Williams gave his partner a sour look and said, "Yeah, okay."

"This way, Mr. Stark," Nurse O'Malley said.

"Thanks," Sangster said to Telemaco, then said, "Thank you," to the doctor.

The detective nodded, and the doctor said, "Yes, of course."

Sangster turned and followed the nurse.

TWO

The nurse swept back a curtain to reveal Ken Burke lying on a gurney, a sheet pulled up to his neck. It was the first time Sangster could remember seeing Burke look his age. He was pale and drawn, the wrinkles were more deeply etched into his face than normal. They added age now, rather than character.

His breathing seemed normal to Sangster, nothing labored about it.

"Just a few minutes, please," Nurse O'Malley said.

"Sure."

She nodded and withdrew.

Sangster stepped closer to his friend and neighbor.

"Burke? Hey, Burke. Can you hear me?"

For a moment there was no reaction, but then the old man's eyes fluttered open.

"Sangster?"

The ex-hitman leaned in closer and said, "Stark."

"Right, right," Burke said, his eyes closing again.

"Hey, old man!" Sangster snapped. "Stay with me!"

Burke's eyes opened, again.

"What happened?"

"M-made a f-fool of myself," Burke said. "Got c-caught."

"What are you talking about, Burke?" Sangster asked,

"T-talk to Polly."

"Polly? Polly who—wait. You mean the woman who cleans your house? That Polly?"

"Talk—talk to P-Polly . . ." Burke said again, and then drifted off.

"What the hell—"

Nurse O'Malley came in, brushed past Sangster, checked Burke's pulse, then looked at the visitor.

"That's enough, I'm afraid," she said, firmly. "We're going to move him to a room. You'll have to speak with Billing."

"Yeah, sure," Sangster said, "but I think I have to talk to the cops, first."

"They're still waiting in the hall for you."

"Okay." He cast one last look at Burke.

"We'll take care of him," she promised.

"But will you find out what's wrong with him?"

"I'm sure the doctors will do their best."

Sangster nodded, then went out to talk to the detectives.

He found Telemaco standing alone.

"Let's go to the cafeteria and get some coffee," the detective said.

"Where's your partner?"

"I sent him to Pirates Alley with some uniforms."

"Pirates Alley?"

"That's where the sheriff was found."

Sangster knew that Telemaco referring to Burke as "the sheriff" was a sign of respect for the old lawman, and he appreciated it.

"Sure," he said, "coffee sounds fine."

They each got a coffee in real cups rather than Styrofoam and took them to a table.

"What was the sheriff up to, Sangster?" Telemaco said, purposely not using "Stark." He had found out

Sangster's name last year, when they were both in Las Vegas. Apparently, he hadn't bothered to fill his partner in.

"I don't know," Sangster said. "He didn't tell me he was up to anything."

"So ya'll don't know what he was doing in Pirates Alley close to midnight?"

"No idea."

"And if ya'll did, you'd tell me, right?"

"Why wouldn't I? I'd like to find out what happened to him."

"You mean you'd like *me* to find out what happened to him, right?" Telemaco said.

"That's what I mean."

"Did he say anything to you just now?"

"Nothing that made any sense," Sangster said, without hesitation. Maybe he didn't kill people for a living anymore, but he was still a pretty damn good liar.

"Like what?"

"He was mumbling," Sangster said. "Said he made a fool of himself, got caught. Not much else."

Telemaco sat back and rubbed his gray-and-black stubble thoughtfully.

"What the hell was he doin', working a case of some kind?" he leaned forward. "Was he doing any P.I. work?"

"No," Sangster said, "not that he told me."

"You guys are tight, right?" Telemaco asked. "He'd tell you a thing like that?"

"Yes, he would."

"Well, we didn't get much out of him, either," the detective admitted. "I'll have to try and talk to him again when they get him into a room. Meanwhile, maybe Williams is finding something helpful."

"Yeah," Sangster said, "maybe."

"I need something from you, Sangster."

"What's that?"

"I need your word you're not gonna get in my way on this."

"Why would I?"

"Because you have a history of takin' things into your own hands. You're not gonna try to deny that, are you? Not after Vegas."

"That was my own business," Sangster said. "This is Burke's business."

"And now it's mine," Telemaco said. "I don't want you in my business."

"Don't worry," Sangster said. "I can safely say the last thing I want to do is get into your business."

Telemaco stared at Sangster intently, as if he was trying to read between the lines.

THREE

Sangster waited around for them to get Burke into a room.

While he was waiting he went and talked to the billing department. He told them he'd get Burke's Medicare information and that the bills for anything not covered should be sent to Burke's address. That was because he didn't want to give out his own.

That done he found out what room Burke was in, took the elevator to the right floor and found him out cold in a bed. There were tubes attached to machines that were beeping, and would keep beeping as long as Burke was breathing.

"Excuse me," a middle-aged nurse said, slipping past him.

"Oh, sorry." He stepped aside.

"Are you family?"

"His friend," Sangster said, "and neighbor."

"You shouldn't be here, then." She went to the machine, checked the connections, and then turned to face him.

"Where's Nurse O'Malley?" he asked.

"She's an emergency room nurse," she answered, "so she's in the emergency room. She's through with this case."

"How is he?"

"Resting," she said. "That's the best thing he can do." She pointed her finger at him. "Five more minutes. Understand?"

"I understand," he said. "Thank you."

She left the room and he walked to the bed. Burke was breathing evenly, the machine beeping rhythmically.

Talk to Polly was all he had. "I need more, old man. Come on, wake up."

He didn't.

"How's he doin'?"

He turned, saw Telemaco standing in the doorway.

"Resting," Sangster said. "They tell me that's the best thing he can do."

"Has he said anything?"

"No," Sangster said. "He hasn't come around."

"And downstairs?"

"I told you what he said when you bought me that great cup of coffee."

"I know," Telemaco said. "I just thought maybe ya'll might have something to add."

"No," Sangster said, "I've got nothing." He turned and looked at Burke. "I was hoping he'd wake up and talk to me."

"Well," the detective said, "I'm gonna leave a man on the door in case he does wake up and say something."

"Or in case somebody wants to hit him on the head, again?"

"Yeah," Telemaco said, "that, too."

"Mind if I keep in touch with you?" Sangster asked. "In case he asks for me?"

"I'd actually prefer that," Telemaco said.

"Fine."

Telemaco started to leave, then stopped.

"You comin'?"

"Yeah," Sangster said, with a last look back at the man in the bed, "I was just leaving."

* * *

Telemaco walked with Sangster to the front door, and out.

"Can I drop you anywhere?" he asked.

"I've got a car," Sangster said.

"Okay, then."

"Where's your partner?"

Telemaco jerked his head toward the curb. There was a Crown Victoria there with Williams behind the wheel.

"Oh," Sangster said, "glad I didn't need that ride."

"I'll see you . . . Stark."

As the detective started away Sangster asked, "Your partner find anything in Pirates Alley?"

Telemaco just waved and kept going.

When he was sure the cops were gone Sangster turned around and went back inside.

He found Nurse Claire O'Malley in the emergency room, standing at the front desk talking to the nurse behind it.

"Mr. . . . ." she said, as he approached.

"Stark," he said. "Can we talk?"

"Sure," she said, "I have a few minutes."

They walked off to one side and stood against a wall. There was plenty of activity going on around them, and no one was paying much attention to them.

Sangster noticed that while she might be called a plain woman, there was still something very attractive about her. Maybe it was the white nurse's uniform. He'd never understood the appeal of the Catholic school girl look, but a nurse . . . well, that was different.

"Can I assume that you're the one who spent the most time with Burke?" he asked.

"Well . . . maybe other than the doctor who actually worked on him."

"Can you tell me if he had any other bruises?"

"Bruises?"

"Yes," Sangster said, "maybe around his ribs, or torso—"

"Are you thinking he might have been beaten?"

"Or kicked, while he was down."

She thought a moment, then said, "No, there was no indication of that. Are you . . . a policeman?"

"Just his friend and neighbor."

"A rather good friend, I'd say, for him to ask for you."

"That's another question," he said. "You told me I was his emergency contact. Did he have something on him, in writing, I mean, to that effect?"

"No," she said, "he told me specifically to call you, and gave me your phone number."

"Was he able to say anything else?"

"Like what?"

"Well, anything that might be helpful in figuring out who did this to him."

"No," she said, "nothing . . . but isn't that the job of the police?"

"Yes, of course," Sangster said, "I'm just trying to be . . . helpful."

"Really?" she asked. "You seem to know what kind of questions to ask."

"I read a lot of mysteries."

She looked at the tiny watch on her wrist.

"I have to go back to work."

"Of course," he said, "thank you for talking to me."

"No problem." She stood there a moment more, then said, "Call me . . ."

"What?"

". . . if you think of anything else you, uh, want to ask me," she finished.

"Oh," he said. "Yes, okay . . . thanks, again."

She nodded. As she walked away he suddenly had the urge to see what she looked like with all those red curls down.

FOUR

He made sure the hospital had his phone number, in case anything went wrong, and left to drive back home to his house in Algiers. He'd return later in the day, during visiting hours, hopefully he'd find something out by then.

When he got home there wasn't much to do except catch a few winks. He removed his shoes, laid down on the bed fully dressed and fell asleep.

He woke several hours later, ravenously hungry. He made himself an egg sandwich, washed it down with two cups of strong coffee. Finishing the last cup, he looked out the window at Burke's house, next door.

Polly was a middle-aged woman who cleaned Burke's house for him. As for his own house, Sangster cleaned it himself, not wanting anyone inside at any time, even though Burke had recommended Polly several times.

He sometimes saw Polly arrive in the morning between eight and nine a.m., other times saw her leave about three or four in the afternoon. However, he didn't know her, or what her exact schedule was. So he wasn't sure if she'd be cleaning Burke's house on this day, but that was the only place he had to start.

He rinsed his empty cup out, grabbed the extra key Burke had given him some time ago, and went next door.

* * *

In the almost four years he had been renting his house on Algiers Point, across Lake Ponchartrain from the French Quarter, he had played chess with Burke at least three times a week. They alternated porches for their games, turning their matches into a home and away series.

The two houses were similar: two story wood-frame structures that had survived both the fire of 1895 and Hurricane Katrina. Sangster rented his, but Burke owned.

Before using the key he knocked, in case Polly was inside cleaning. When there was no answer he used the key to let himself in.

Burke also had an extra key to Sangster's house, but it had taken the two men a long time to trust each other that much. Sangster, the ex-hitman, had been shocked to find that Burke, the ex-lawman, was a kindred spirit, and the two had formed a bond—the kind of bond Sangster had never experienced, and never could have experienced, before that morning when he woke to find that he suddenly had a soul.

It took only seconds to ascertain that Polly was not around. However, the house was clean, so he assumed she had been there in the past day or so.

There wasn't much he could do for his friend until he spoke with Polly. That meant finding her. Burke had a small office, with a desk and one file cabinet. Sangster went through the cabinet. In the first drawer he discovered Sheriff's Department files, all of them unsolved cases. But he wasn't interested in those at the moment. In the second drawer he found what he wanted: copies of paid—and unpaid—bills. He had to go through gas, electric, mortgage and other monthly bills before finding some canceled checks that had been written to Polly. He pulled the folder out, leafed through it, and finally found Polly's address. He didn't recognize the street, but it was also an Algiers address. He kept the piece of paper it was written on and returned the file to the cabinet. Then he left Burke's house, locking the door behind him.

He went back to his house, using his landline to call the hospital and check on Burke's condition. A woman at the nurse's station told him Mr. Burke's condition had not change—no better, no worse.

"Can you tell me if there is still a policeman outside his door?" he asked.

"Yes, sir, there is."

"Thank you."

He hung up. There was no reason for him to rush to the hospital right away. So, he decided to go find Polly, and then see Burke during the evening visiting hours.

After locking up his house, Sangster set off on foot to find Polly.

Algiers was home to many pubs and restaurants—no fast food places allowed—many of which, like the Old Point Bar, had live music. Some of the Mardi-Gras troupes had warehouses there. In addition, there were many Catholic and Baptist churches in the area. The population was about 2,200.

As Sangster walked, he discovered that Evelina Ave, where Polly lived, was also in Algiers Point, but on the other side of the ferry landing. When he reached the address he saw it was one of the older shotgun style houses, so-called because there were no hallways inside. You could fire a shotgun through the front door and the bullet would come out the back door.

He stepped up to the front door and knocked. After a few moments the door was answered by a small boy about eight.

"Hello," he said, looking up at Sangster.

"Hello," Sangster said, "does Polly Bourque live here?"

"Yeah," the boy said, "she's my ma. I'm Hugo."

"Hugo, is your ma home?"

"Naw," the boy said, "she's at work."

"Work?"

"She cleans."

"Are you here alone?"

"Naw," Hugo said. "My sister's here."

"Is she older than you, or younger?"

"She's older."

"Can I talk to her?"

Instead of answering, the boy turned and ran back inside the house, yelling, "Octavia!"

Sangster waited and after a few moments a teenage girl wearing tank top and cut offs, came to the door. She was dark-skinned, pretty, with pointy little tits and not an ounce of fat on her. She looked him up and down, pushing her pokies out at him.

"Where y'at?" was the traditional New Orleans greeting, only she said, "Where YOU at?"

"What it is," he said, giving the standard response.

The girl smiled and said, "You ain't no Algerine."

"No, I'm not," he said. "I'm looking for your mother."

"Why?"

"A friend of hers is in the hospital," Sangster said. "I just want to let her know."

"I can tell 'er."

"I'd like to tell her myself," he responded. "Where she is?"

"She's workin'."

"Your little brother told me that much. Can you tell me where?"

"It's Tuesday, so I think today she's doin' the schools."

"The schools?"

"Yeah," the girl said. "She cleans a couple of the schools."

"Which ones?"

"I think she's on Old Aurora today," she said. "That'd be Alice M. Harte Elementary or Edna Karr High."

Sangster didn't know the schools in Algiers, but he could find them.

"Thanks for the information, Octavia."

She cocked her head to one side and said, "You wanna maybe come in, have a drink?"

"How old are you?"

"Eighteen."

"Yeah, sure," he said. "Call me in four or five years, Sweetheart."

As he walked away he heard her say, "Chicken."

FIVE

He tried the Elementary school first. School was out for the summer, so he had to bang on a few doors before somebody answered.

"Sorry," a man in grey overalls said, "she ain't workin' here today."

"Okay, thanks."

The schools were in the same zip code, about a mile and a half apart. He walked to Edna Karr High and went through the motions of banging on doors again. This time instead of a janitor in grey, a pretty brunette of about thirty opened the door, peered at him over the frame of her glasses. She was slender, with creamy skin and a fresh, clean smell all over her.

"Can I help you?" she asked.

"Sorry to bother you," he said. "But I'm looking for a lady name Polly Bourque, I understand she cleans here?"

"Polly, yes," the woman said. "She does, but . . . who are you?"

"I'm a friend—well, a friend of someone she works for. My neighbor. He's in the hospital and wanted me to tell her. I went to her house and her daughter, Octavia, told me she was here."

He threw in Octavia's name, just in case the woman might know it.

"Octavia, yes, attends school here. She's a student of mine."

"Well," Sangster said, "could you take me to Polly? Or have her come out here? Either one works for me, whichever you're more comfortable with."

"Are you a policeman?" she asked.

"No," he said. "Why would ask me that?"

"There's just something . . . authoritative about you."

"Really? Well, I guess I'll take that as a compliment."

"Why don't you come in," she said. "I'll show you where she is."

"Thanks."

He hadn't been inside a school in many, many years, but this one brought back memories. He guessed that walking the halls of any school would have done that. Even the smell was familiar.

"I thought teachers were off when the schools were out for summer," he said.

"Oh, I will be," she said. "I just have some paperwork to clean up."

"What do you teach?"

"History and Music."

"Music," he said. "I never had a music teacher as pretty as you."

"I guess I'll take that as a compliment," she said. "Polly's in here. At least, she was a little while ago. Ah, yes, there she is."

They were outside a pair of double doors that opened to a cafeteria. Inside he could see a black woman cleaning the floors with a mop.

"Shall I come in with you?" the teacher asked.

"What's your name?" he asked.

"Oh, I'm sorry. My name is Andrea Karlson—Miss Karlson."

"My name's Stark," he said. "Why don't you do that, Miss Karlson? Come in with me so I don't startle her."

"Very well, Mr. Stark. That sounds like a good idea."

She opened the door and they went in.

Polly looked up, stopped what she was doing and leaned on her mop. She was wearing a shapeless dress and a kerchief on her head.

"Miss Karlson," she said. "Can I he'p you?"

"This man is looking for you, Polly," Andrea Karlson said. "His name is Mr. Stark."

"Mr. Stark?" Polly peered at him. "Do I know you?"

"Kind of," Sangster said. "I'm Ken Burke's neighbor."

"Dat's right," Polly said. "I seen you there. Why you lookin' fer me?"

"I need to talk to you, Polly," he said. "It's about Burke."

They both looked at Andrea Karlson.

"Well," the teacher said, "I guess I'll leave you to it. Polly, will you show Mr. Stark out when you're finished?"

"Of course, Miss Karlson."

"Mr. Stark, nice to meet you."

"And you."

Andrea left the cafeteria.

"She's a nice lady," Polly said.

"She seems like it," Sangster said. "Polly, Burke's in the hospital."

"What? Why?"

"Someone attacked him in the French Quarter."

"Is he all right?"

"Can we sit down?"

All the chairs were up on top of the tables.

"Sure," she said, "take down two chairs."

He took them down and they sat.

"Is Burke all right?"

"He was hit on the head," Sangster said. "He's actually okay physically, but he's pretty much in and out of consciousness. The doctors don't know why."

"What did Burke say?" she asked.

"So far he's only said one thing to me," Sangster answered. "'Talk to Polly.'"

She bit her lip.

"What's this about, Polly?" Sangster asked. "Was he doing something for you?"

She didn't answer, but starred to worry her bottom lip.

"Polly," he said, "if Burke was helping you with something he can't help you now. But maybe you can help him."

"How?"

Sangster leaned forward, elbows on his knees, and lowered his voice for effect.

"Tell me what he was doing, Polly."

SIX

"All right," she said. "It's about my daughter."

"Octavia?"

"No," Polly said, "I got another daughter, Isola. She's seventeen."

"And how old is Octavia?"

"Fourteen. Hugo, he nine."

"Okay," Sangster said, "what's going on with Isola?"

"She got herself involved in somet'in' bad," Polly said.

"Like what?"

"I don't know," she said. "Dat's what Burke was supposed ta find out."

"Come on, Polly," Sangster said. "You must've given him something to go on."

"Isola, she hang out with dese girls in the Quarter," Polly said. "Dey bad girls."

"Bad in what way?"

"Dey don't got no parents," Polly said. "And dey involved in . . ."

"I know," Sangster said, "bad things. Don't make me drag this out of you, Polly."

She hesitated a moment, then said, "Gris-gris."

Sangster heard that phrase before.

"Voodoo?" he asked.

She nodded, looking frightened

"Polly, do you believe in Voodoo?"

When she nodded it was a jerky motion.

"And you told this to Burke?"

"Yes."

"What did he say?"

"He say he gon' prove to me dere ain't no such t'ing," she said. "He gon' save my Isola from it."

"How was he going to do that?"

"I don't know."

Sangster paused to think for a minute. He wanted to help Burke, but did he want to get involved in everything that went along with this mumbo-jumbo?

"You say he don' wake up?"

"Not much," he said, still thinking.

"That could be . . . Hoodoo," she said, lowering her voice.

"What?"

"Maybe he been put a spell on," she said, "a Hood-doo spell."

"Is there a difference between Voodoo and Hoo-doo?" he asked.

"Hoo-doo be part of Voodoo," she said. "It got to do with . . . with conjuration."

"Spells."

She nodded.

"So Burke didn't believe in this stuff."

"No, but he say he gon' help my girl."

"And that's what he was doing in the Quarter."

"Dat where dem girls hang around," Polly said.

"Do they live there?"

"Yes."

"And you believe they practice . . . Voodoo there?" he asked.

She nodded.

"What makes you think Isola was involved with it?"

"I find some jimson weed in her room."

"What's that got to do with Voodoo?"

"It used to cast spells."

"Could she have had it for another reason?"

"I don't know."

"Anything else?"

She nodded jerkily, again, her face etched with fear.

"What?"

"A doll."

"A Voodoo doll?"

She nodded.

"I find it in her room, after she gone."

"Isola's gone?"

"Yeah," she said, "dat why I finally tol' Burke about it. He see I upset one day, and he ast me."

"How long has she been gone?"

"A week."

"And when did you tell Burke?"

"Two days ago."

So Burke had been working on this for two days. That figured. He hadn't been available for chess but he wouldn't say why.

"What about Octavia?" he asked.

"What about her?'

"Is she involved in any of this stuff?"

"I don't t'ink so."

"Is she close with her sister?"

"Not close, no."

"Polly, forgive me, but Octavia strikes me as being kind of wild."

Polly nodded. "She wild, but she not into Voodoo."

"What makes you say that?"

"She t'ink it stupid. Octavia, she may be wild, but she a smart girl."

"And Isola? Is she smart?"

"Not so smart," Polly admitted. "Not like Octavia."

"They're three years apart?"

She nodded. Then she asked, "She make eyes at you?"

Sangster assumed she was asking if the girl had flirted with him.

"Yes, she did."

Polly shook her head. "Wild."

"What about Hugo?"

"He a good boy," she said. "And smart."

"How close is he with his sisters?"

"Close with Isola," she said, "not so much with 'Tavia."

Sangster wondered if Polly was really a good judge of how close her children were with each other.

"All right, Polly," he said, "we'll talk again."

"Whatchoo gon' do, Mr. Stark?"

"I need to find out who did this to Burke," he said.

"Dat mean you gon' help me and my girl?"

He hesitated, then said, "I guess it does."

"Burke say you a good friend."

"When did he say that?"

"All de time."

"That's good to know."

"You take me to see him?" she asked.

"Sure," he said. "When do you want to go?"

"Now."

"You can leave, just like that?"

"I my own boss."

"Okay, then."

"I get changed," she said, standing up. "Dese my work clothes."

Before she could leave the room Sangster said, "Polly?"

"Yeah?"

"If you don't mind me asking," he said, "why would Burke be willing to help you like this?"

"He a good man—" she said.

"Well—"

"—and he's my man."

SEVEN

Sangster and Polly took the ferry from Algiers to Canal Street. That meant they traveled from the second oldest city in New Orleans to the oldest—but only by a year, 1718 to 1719.

When Sangster got to the hospital with Polly, Burke was still unconscious. Polly pulled a chair up to his bed and sat.

"Has he said anything?" Sangster asked the police officer.

"No, Mr. Stark, not a word," the young cop said.

Telemaco had left Stark's name at the desk, with orders that he was allowed to see Burke. There were no other names on the list, but since Polly was with Sangster she was allowed in.

"Okay, thanks."

"The nurse said the doctor would be by in a few," the cop said. "That was a while ago."

"Again, thanks."

He went into the room, put his hand on Polly's shoulder.

"I been talkin' to him," she said, "but he don't hear."

"Maybe he does."

"What da doctor say?" she asked.

"The cop says he's supposed to be here, soon," Sangster said. "We'll ask him."

Polly squeezed Burke's hand.

"You an ol' fool," she told him.

"Polly," Sangster warned, "he might be able to hear you."

"He still an ol' fool."

Sangster walked to the door to wait for the doctor. After another "few" he showed up. It was the tall, skinny Doctor Judd.

"Mr. . . ." he said.

"Stark," Sangster said. "How is he?"

"Why don't we go inside," the doctor said.

Polly turned, saw the doctor and stood up.

"Doc, this is Polly. She's Burke's . . . friend."

"Another friend?" the doctor said, with a crooked grin. "He's a lucky man."

"Is he?" Sangster asked.

"Well . . . no."

"What's going on?" Sangster asked.

"Damned if we know," Dr. Judd said. "According to his vital signs he should be up and around by now."

Polly stole a "I told you so" look toward Sangster.

"So what are you doing about it?"

"What else can we do, Mr. Stark?" the doctor asked. "More tests. Unless you have a suggestion?"

"Me? I'm not a doctor."

"Then you see how puzzled we are," Doctor Judd said. "I'll take a suggestion from a laymen."

Polly gave Sangster a look, again.

"No," Sangster said, "I don't have any suggestions— at least, not at the moment."

"All right, then," Judd said. "I just need to check his vitals, and then I'm going to schedule him for more tests."

"We'll go get some lunch, or something."

"You just need to step out for a few moments," Judd told him.

"We'll be back," Sangster said. He took Polly's arm and guided her into the hall. "Are you hungry?"

"I'm always hungry," she told him. "That what Burke says, anyway."

"They have a cafeteria, or we could go out."

"Here is fine with me."

"Okay," he said. "Let's go get something and talk."

"Yes."

He went to take her elbow again, but this time she pulled it away, folded her arms.

"Sorry."

"Let's just go."

Neither of them ordered food. Sangster got a cup of coffee, and Polly tea.

"You wanted me to tell the doctor about the . . . the Voodoo, didn't you?"

"He ast you for a suggestion."

"I know."

"You heard what he say. Burke don't have no reason to be like dis, but he is."

"And your only suggestion is Voodoo."

"Mr. Stark," she said, "dat is de whole reason Burke got involved."

"But he was trying to prove to you that Voodoo's not involved . . . wasn't he?"

"Maybe."

Since she had changed her clothes she had lost about ten years on his estimate of her age. He now figured her for her late forties. Burke was in his seventies.

"What other reason you got for his condition?" she asked.

"None," he admitted. "Not now. Not yet. Could you tell anything from looking at him?"

"I tol' you I believe in Voodoo," she said. "I don't practice it. I can't tell nothin' by lookin' at him."

"Who can?"

"A Voodoo priest."

"Do you know one we can have look at him?" He

didn't believe he had asked that question.

"I don't know anybody," she said. "I—I don't wan' to know dose people."

"But Isola does, right?"

"Yes."

He sat back in his chair.

"Okay," he said, "maybe I need to talk to someone who knows this subject."

"Not a priest?"

"Not yet," he said. "Maybe some kind of an expert."

"Like . . . a teacher?"

"A teacher," he said, "A professor. Somebody's who's studied the subject. Yeah, that'd work."

She thought a moment before speaking.

"I know somebody."

"You do?" He leaned forward. "Who?"

"Miss Karlson."

"Karlson . . . the history teacher at the school?"

She nodded.

"History," she said. "She teaches local history, and dat includes . . ."

". . . Voodoo."

Polly nodded.

He scratched the stubble on his face and said, "That may not be a bad idea."

"Do you want me ta ask her?"

"No," Sangster said, "I'll do that. But I do have some more questions for you."

"Ask dem."

"What's your daughter's interest in Voodoo?" he asked. "How did that start? Is it because you're from here?"

"I am Jamaican," she said. "My family come here when I was about Isola's age."

"And your kids?"

"Dey was all born here."

"Do they all have the same fathers?"

"No," she said, "Hugo has a different one."

"Are either of them still around?"

"No."

"Okay, so Jamaica," he said. "Voodoo is practiced there, too, isn't it?"

"Sure it is," she said, "and dere ain't so very big a difference. I mean, dere are some differences, but in lots of ways dey's also alike."

"Well," Sangster said, "I guess Miss Karlson can help me with the differences."

Quinlan had rented a car by this time, and when Sangster drove to the ferry with the black woman and rode across, he followed. Sangster must have been out of practice, because he didn't seem to know he had a tail. Quinlan followed them to the hospital, remained in the parking lot when they went inside. He got out, leaned against the car, and lit up a cigarette. He did not once wonder why Sangster was going into a hospital.

Patience was a hitman's biggest ally.

EIGHT

Sangster took Polly back up to Burke's room so she could sit with him for a while. He left her there and walked to the waiting area next to a couple of prospective fathers. He avoided conversation with them and they eventually talked around him.

He was still sitting there half an hour later when Detective Telemaco came in.

"Mr. Stark," he said. "Where y'at? Mind if I sit?"

"Not at all."

Telemaco sat next to him. Across from them two fathers-to-be were still deep in conversation.

"What's with them?"

"Prospective fathers," Sangster said, "comparing notes."

"And ya'll?" Telemaco asked. "What are ya'll doin' here?"

"I brought a friend to see Burke."

"Who's that?"

"His housekeeper."

"That's nice."

"Yeah, it is. Where's your partner?"

"Working."

"And you're what? Just paying a friendly visit?"

"I wanted to see if Burke was awake, or if he said anything."

"Well, according to your man on the door, he hasn't said a word."

"Maybe he's talked to his housekeeper."

"We can ask her," Sangster said, "but the doctor

doesn't seem to think that's possible."

"What did he have to say?"

"They still don't know why he's unconscious. They're going to do more tests."

"Jesus," Telemaco said, shaking his head, "doctors and their tests."

"Yeah."

A nurse appeared and approached the two prospective fathers. She said one of their names, but the both of them got very excited and hugged each other. Then one of them was led away. The other one sat and beamed at Sangster and Telemaco.

"Maybe we should go and find out," Telemaco said. "It's probably close to the end of visiting hours."

When they entered the room Polly turned her head and looked up at them. She was holding Burke's hand.

"Has he said anything?" Sangster asked.

"No," she said, "not a word."

"Too bad," Telemaco said. "Has he even opened his eyes?"

"No," she said. "He ain't moved a bit."

"I suppose I better talk to the doctor," Telemaco said. "Judd, isn't it?"

"That's right."

Telemaco nodded. "See ya'll later."

As the detective left, Sangster asked Polly, "Was that the truth? He hasn't talked or moved?"

"He is very deep," she said.

"In a coma?" Sangster asked. "Is that what the doctor said?"

"No, I don't t'ink it is a coma."

"Oh," Sangster said, "you're saying it's a . . . spell."

She nodded.

"Okay—"

He was cut off by the appearance of a nurse.

"I'm sorry," she said. "Visiting hours are over. You'll have to leave."

"Okay," Sangster said. "Thank you. Come on, Polly."

Polly released Burke's hand and stood up.

"Nurse, can you tell me what kind of coma he's in?" Sangster asked.

"Actually, I can't," she said.

"I just need to—"

"No," she said, "I can't, because it's unlike anything we've ever seen before."

He looked at Polly, who raised her eyebrows.

"We'll get out of your way now."

She adjusted Burke's pillows and sheet and said, "Come back and see him tomorrow."

"We will."

Sangster took Polly's elbow. This time she didn't jerk away.

They left the hospital without running into Telemaco again, which suited Sangster just fine.

"I'll take you back to Algiers," Sangster said, when they were out front.

"What will you be doin'?"

"I guess I'm going to have to try to find your daughter," he said, "Isola."

"Why would you do dat?" she asked. "Why do you want to help me?"

"To tell the truth," he said, "I don't. I want to find out who did this to Burke. I think the best way to do that is to find Isola."

She nodded and said, "Thank you for tellin' me da trut'."

"Polly," he said, "while I'm looking for the attacker,

I'll do my best to help your daughter, too."

"I appreciate dat, Mr. Stark."

"Just . . . call me Stark. No mister."

"Stark."

"All right," Sangster said. "Do you think your daughter Octavia will be home?"

"She better be," Polly said. "She supposed to be watchin' her brother."

"Okay, good," he said. "I want to speak with both of them."

NINE

Sangster stopped his car in front of Polly's house. They had ridden from the hospital in silence. He turned and looked at her. Her profile was grim, but her skin was smooth, the color of coffee-with-cream. Sangster could see why Burke was attracted to her. She was a good-looking woman.

"What about your children's father?" he asked.

"Dead," she said, "a long time—and he weren't much of a man when he was alive."

"I'll come in with you and speak with your daughter, if that's all right," he said.

"If Octavia has done what she supposed to, dinner will be ready," she said. "You can eat with us."

His first instinct was to refuse, but he had second thoughts and said, "Fine. Thanks."

They walked to the front door and when she opened it he smelled the food cooking. Apparently, Octavia had done her job, after all.

"Mama's home!" Hugo shouted, running to her.

"Hello, my beautiful boy," Polly said, crouching down to hug him.

"He was here before, Mama," Hugo said, pointing over her shoulder at Sangster.

"Hello, Hugo."

"Hugo, this is Mr. Stark," Polly said. "He's a friend."

"Just call me Stark, Hugo."

Polly stood up.

"It smells like your sister cooked, like I asked her to."

"She did," Hugo said. "She made etouffee."

"I thought she'd make something Jamaican."

"I'm from Jamaica, but my children were born and brought up here."

All three of them went to the kitchen, where Octavia was standing in front of the stove. She was still dressed as she had been when Sangster saw her, which meant she was barely covered. He could see the resemblance between her and her mother.

"It's almost ready, Mommy," she said, over her shoulder.

"We have a guest, 'Tavia," her mother announced.

This time the girl gave Sangster a long look, then said to her mother, "There's plenty. We just need to set another place."

"I'll do it!" Hugo shouted.

"Good boy," Polly said. "I want to freshen up." She looked at Sangster. "I'll show you to the bathroom so you can wash up."

"Thank you."

"Ten minutes!" Octavia announced.

"We be ready," Polly promised.

Sangster followed her out of the kitchen.

Octavia was a good cook.

Sangster hadn't had such good etouffe since last year. He'd been found by his past in Algiers and forced to kill again to protect himself and others. Now he had to lay low, keep his head down, which meant more home cooked meals, or eating out only in Algiers Point.

"This was great, Octavia," he said.

"Would you like some more?" Polly asked, when Octavia did not respond.

"No, I've had plenty, thanks," Sangster said. He looked across the table at Hugo, who was still shoveling it in. Apparently the very definition of a growing boy, he was, however, very skinny, like most kids his age Sangster saw on the streets of Algiers.

"Hugo," Polly said, standing up, "you are going to help me with de dishes, boy."

"Aw, Ma that's for girl—"

"Don't sass me, boy," Polly said. "Your sister has to spend some time talking with Stark." She looked at Sangster. "You can use the living room, or the porch."

"My room would be more private," Octavia pointed out.

"No boys in your room, my girl," Polly said. "Dat includes grown men."

Octavia rolled her eyes at Sangster.

"The porch, then," she said.

"Suits me."

"I'll bring coffee out later," Polly said. "Jamaican Blue Mountain."

"Sounds good."

Octavia had already left the kitchen. When Sangster joined her on the porch she was smoking a cigarette. The tip of it glowed in the dark.

"Your mother know about that particular vice?" he asked.

"No," Octavia said, blowing out a stream of smoke. Sangster doubted she was even inhaling. It was all for show. "Are you gonna tell her?"

"None of my business," Sangster said. "You want to ruin your health and turn your teeth yellow, be my guest."

Octavia looked at the cigarette in her hand, then tossed it away into the night.

"What do you want with me, Stark?"

"Just a few questions."

"About what?"

"Your sister, Isola."

"Isola is stuck up."

"That may be," Sangster said, "but I think she's the only one who can help me find out who hurt my friend, Burke."

She laughed. "My mother's old boyfriend?"

"My friend," Sangster said. "That's all I care about. If you intend to bad mouth him, we're going to have a problem."

She turned to face him with her chin high and her pointy little tits thrust out at him.

"No problem, Stark."

"Do you know where your sister is?"

"No."

"Do you know the girls she hangs out with?"

"Some of them."

"Will you give me their names and addresses?"

She shrugged, allowed his shoulders to slump. "Why not?"

"Okay. You can give me a written list before I leave tonight."

"Anything else?"

"How much do you know about your sister's involvement with Voodoo?"

"Enough to know I don't want any part of it," she said.

"Why is that?"

"Because she is involved with Haitian Voodoo," Octavia said. "Our heritage is Creole Voodoo."

"So which one do you believe in?"

"Neither. I just think if Isola is gonna be stupid, she should be stupid the right way."

"The Jamaican way."

Octavia nodded.

The front door opened and Polly came out carrying a mug of coffee. The scent was mild Jamaican Blue Mountain brew, not like the stronger New Orleans

Roast, laced with chicory.

"Thank you, Polly," Sangster said, accepting the mug.

"Any problems out here?" she asked.

"No," he said, "no problems. Octavia's being very helpful."

Polly looked at her daughter, sniffed the night air and asked, "Girl, you been smokin'?"

Before the girl could say anything Sangster said, "No, she hasn't been."

"She better not."

Polly went back inside.

"I'll write those names and addresses down for you," Octavia said.

"Thanks. I appreciate it."

She followed her mother back inside. Sangster remained on the porch and sipped his Jamaican coffee.

Quinlan parked down the block from the house Sangster and the black woman had gone into. For a moment he wondered if Sangster was tapping the woman. She might have been a little old, but she seemed to have a fine, sturdy body. It didn't really matter. All he was trying to determine was whether or not Sangster had a routine. Maybe he came to this lady's house for dinner every night.

This time when he lit a cigarette he remained in the car. He'd be less noticeable that way.

TEN

Sangster returned home, went to the desk in his living room, turned on the light and sat there studying the slip of paper Octavia had given him. Three names, and three addresses. The zip code on all three was the same. What were three Garden District girls doing with a girl from Algiers? Apparently, leading her down the garden path—but to where?

Octavia had also given Sangster another address. It was a Voodoo shop in the French Quarter. Looked like his vow to stay out of the Quarter as much as he could was going to go by the boards.

He got up from the desk and stopped short. Something wasn't right. He studied the desk, then looked around him. His environment had been disturbed, somehow. What bothered him was how long it had taken to notice. He was out of practice.

Someone had been in the house. They'd gone through his desk, moved a few things. Burglars, or somebody from his past? There was no way to know. He walked the rest of the house. Just a few things had been disturbed. But no one was there at the moment, and they hadn't left anything behind.

He checked his watch, saw that it was almost eleven. He folded the slip of paper, put it in his pocket, turned off the desk lamp and left the house.

Sangster didn't know the exact count but there were several Catholic and Baptist churches in Algiers Point.

Tonight he was going to visit the Holy Name of St. Mary Catholic Church on Eliza Street.

Since the morning he woke to find that he had a soul, Sangster had been struggling with what it meant. He wasn't even quite sure of what a soul was.

In Las Vegas last year, he'd spent time with an Obeah Man discussing the soul. Recently he'd decided to make use of the churches in Algiers Point to try and find someone who could really explain it to him.

Sometimes called "The Cathedral of the West Bank," the church was probably the most impressive single structure in Algiers. It was also the first Roman Catholic church in New Orleans.

Sangster had visited two of the Baptist churches in Algiers so far, but the two Ministers he had spoken to hadn't been able to answer his questions. Tonight he would see if the Catholics could do any better.

The church was open until 12:30 a.m., so he had plenty of time. He walked from his house. The streets pf Algiers were quiet at night, especially away from the clubs and cafes.

Before long the structure of Holy Name stretched out above him with the moon behind it. The spires of the Cathedral were timeless.

He mounted the steps to the front door and entered. The inside was dim, but impressive. The stained glass was breathtaking, especially the one above the huge altar.

He walked down the center aisle, his footsteps echoing. The pews were all empty, but when he stopped moving he heard other footsteps, as well. Suddenly, a man came out from one side of the altar, stopping when he saw Sangster standing there.

"Hello," he said. "There's no mass tonight, my son."

"That's okay," Sangster said. "I wouldn't know what to do during one."

"Not Catholic?" the priest asked.

"No, sir."

The man came down the steps from the altar, stood with his hands behind his back. He was wearing the long black cassock and white collar of his profession. He had the look of an athlete rather than a priest—an athlete just past his prime.

"Then what can we do for you?"

"We?"

"The Church," the priest said. "God."

"Well," Sangster said, "I'm not sure either of you can help me, Father."

"Maybe you should have a seat in one of the pews and we can talk about it. I mean, I assume you came here to talk to . . . somebody."

Sangster stared at the man, looked at the statues on the altar behind him.

"No harm in talking," he said.

"Please." The priest pointed, indicating a pew.

Sangster walked over and sat down. The priest sat in the pew in front of him.

"What's your name, my son?" he asked.

Sangster hesitated, then said, "Stark." He'd been lying about it for so long no point in telling the truth now. "And you?"

"I'm Father Patrick. Mr. Stark, do you live in Algiers?"

"I do. And it's just Stark."

"But you're not a Catholic," Father Patrick said. "Can I ask you where you worship?"

"Nowhere, at the moment."

"Ah, so maybe you're lookin' for someplace?"

"I think," Sangster said, "I'm looking for some answers, rather than a place to actually worship."

"Answers about what?"

"Souls."

"Any souls in particular?"

"Just in general," Sangster said. "I mean, like, what they're for, where they come from, what they do, that sort of thing."

"Those are all good questions," Father Patrick said, "and we actually have some classes that would help—"

"I don't really have time to take classes, Father," Sangster said. "I just thought maybe you could kind of . . . fill me in?"

"Tonight?" Father Patrick asked. "Mr. Stark, it would take more than one night to explain to a man the existence of his soul."

"Whoa, wait a minute," Sangster said. "I didn't say anything about my soul, I said—"

"I know, I know," Father Patrick said, "the soul in general. Still . . . that's not something I'd attempt to tackle in one night. Perhaps we can make some appointments, you could come by the rectory—"

"Maybe," Sangster said, "I could just sit here a while, then. I'll think about making an appointment later on."

"Well," Father Patrick said, "I do have some additional work to do, and I'm not scheduled to close up for about another hour."

"An hour would be good," Sangster said.

"I'll leave you to it, then," the priest said, standing up. "I just need to clean up. I'll try not to bother you while you're . . . thinking."

"Thank you, Father."

The priest nodded and went back to his business.

Sangster sat in silence for the better part of the hour, eyeing all the statuary and stained glass, waiting for some sort of epiphany to strike him. Maybe the priest would be able to explain it all to him over the course of a few meetings, but he had other things to do, at the moment.

Father Patrick moved in and out during that time, removing certain items from the altar and carrying them away with him to the sacristy.

Finally, he reappeared in front of Sangster and said, "I'm afraid it's time for me to close up."

"No problem," Sangster said. "I was just about ready to leave. I do have one other question for you, though."

"And that would be?"

"Do you know anything about Voodoo, Father?"

ELEVEN

The last thing Sangster would have expected that night would have been sitting in a bar after midnight, having a beer with a priest.

But there they were.

He waited outside the church for Father Patrick to change his clothes and lock up. When he came out he was wearing a short-sleeved shirt, and jeans, no collar.

"Isn't that against the Church law, or something?" Sangster asked, touching his own neck.

"Naw," Father Patrick said. "Sometimes it's a little tight. I like to get out and let loose."

Sangster couldn't imagine what a priest's take of "cutting loose" would be, but assumed he would find out.

They went to the Old Point Bar on Patterson Dr. It was late and there was no live music. They got a table and a pint each.

"I didn't think you'd have a beer," Sangster said.

"What'd you expect?" Father Patrick asked. "Sacramental wine?"

"I don't know, Father."

"Look, Stark," the priest said, "why don't you just call me Patrick?"

"Isn't that like a sin, or something?"

"No," Patrick said, "it's my name. Now, what's this about Voodoo? You're interested in souls and Voodoo? That sounds like an odd combination."

"Is it?" Sangster asked.

Patrick shrugged. "Okay, maybe not."

"After all, isn't Voodoo a religion?"

"So they say."

"You don't believe it?"

"I recognize that there are many other religions, but as a Catholic priest I believe in only one God."

"So that makes everyone else's God a false one?"

"In the eyes of the Church, yes," Patrick said. "And by that I mean, in the eyes of a non-progressive Church."

"So you're saying that while the Church itself may be non-progressive, you're a progressive priest."

"Let's just say I don't necessarily toe the party line."

"Doesn't that get you into trouble?"

Patrick laughed. "Frequently."

"So the slant I get from you on the human soul would be different from the one the Church itself believes."

"Sometimes," Patrick said, "what the Church believes and what it teaches are two different things."

Sangster suddenly got the definite feeling he wouldn't be able to get any help from the Catholic Church. Not when it was having problems of its own.

"What about all this stuff in the press about priests and sex?" he asked—mostly to see if he could get a rise out of the man.

"I'm sure it's happened," Patrick said. "Me, I prefer sex with grown women."

"What?"

"I'm forty-eight, Stark," Patrick said. "I've only been in the priesthood for about eighteen years."

"So you've had sex, then."

Patrick drank from his pint and then set the glass down gently. "Lots of it—just not in the past eighteen years."

"What made you become a priest at thirty?" Sangster asked.

"An epiphany," Patrick said. "Have you ever had an epiphany, Stark?"

"Yes," Sangster said. "How has that worked out for you?"

"Well," Patrick said, "I'm still just a parish priest."

"No advancement?"

"I always seem to be putting my foot in my mouth," Patrick said.

"Then maybe I came to church on the wrong night."

"Or," Patrick said, "maybe on the right one."

They had a second pint each and Patrick asked, "What about your epiphany? How has that worked out for you?"

"It's only been about four years," Sangster said. "The jury's still out."

"And did it have something to do with souls, or Voodoo?"

"Voodoo is a very recent interest," Sangster said.

"Souls, then," Patrick said. "That's why you still have questions."

Sangster took a drink.

"You know," Patrick said, "I think maybe the usual classes wouldn't help you very much."

"No?"

"No," Patrick said. "I think you might need some one-on-one counseling."

"You're not making a pass at me, are you, Patrick?"

The priest smiled.

"Remember what I said about full grown women?"

"Yes."

"So . . . we could do it right here, if you like," Patrick said. "Over a pint or two. Just sit and talk about souls. Your soul."

"That's a possibility," Sangster said, "but why don't

we talk about Voodoo tonight."

"I actually don't know that much about it," Patrick said. "Spells and potions and dolls . . . even to a progressive priest it sounds like a bunch of nonsense."

"Why'd you come out for a drink, then?"

"How long have you been here? In Algiers?"

"A few years."

"I've only been here a few months," Patrick said. "I consider myself in exile."

"Big mouth?"

"Again," Patrick said, with a nod. "Monsignor hardly talks to me, the parishioners prefer him, and I don't have many friends. Tonight you just struck me as somebody I'd like to have a pint with. I actually thought we might be able to help each other."

"I'm not looking for any friends, Patrick," Sangster said.

"We don't need to be friends, Stark."

"All right, then." After a moment he asked, "Do you play chess?"

Quinlan heard that Sangster had left the business. Hitmen did that for a variety of reasons. Either they made enough money to retire, lost their taste for it, or got too old to do it anymore. But he had never heard of a hitman getting religion.

There was a first time for everything.

TWELVE

Before going to the French Quarter on Wednesday, Sangster decided to talk to the teacher, Miss Karlson.

He went to Edna Karr High, hoping that Miss Karlson wouldn't have started her vacation yet.

The night before he had asked Polly if she wanted a ride to the hospital. She said she had to work, but that she'd get herself to there that evening for visiting hours. By work he didn't know if she'd meant she'd have to be here, at Karr, to finish up.

He had to bang on the door a second time before it was opened, this time by a man in a grey janitor's jumper.

"We're closed," the man said, mildly annoyed.

"I'm supposed to meet Miss Karlson," Sangster said. "We're, uh, supposed to talk about my son's grades."

"Uh-huh," the janitor said. He was a bored, faded looking man in his sixties, and clearly couldn't care less. "You might as well come in, then. You know where to find her?"

Sangster took a shot and said, "The music department."

"Right. Know where that is?"

"I can wander around and find it."

The man rolled his eyes, assumed a put-upon expression and said, "Come on, I'll show ya."

"Thanks."

The Janitor led him down several halls until they reached a door with a sign that said MUSIC DEPARTMENT.

"There ya go," the man said, and left.

Sangster went in. He saw chairs set up for a band or orchestra, with a podium he assumed was for a conductor. But there was no sign of Miss Karlson. He walked further into the room, thought he heard something being moved, walked to another doorway that appeared to lead to a room filled with instruments.

"Hello?" He knocked, not wanting to frighten her.

"Yes?" her voice came from inside. "Who is it?"

"It's Stark," Sangster said. "I was here yesterday?"

She appeared from around a corner, wearing a sleeveless top, jeans, running shoes, her hair up in a ponytail, and holding a clipboard. She looked extremely fit, like a runner or a tennis player.

"Oh, yes," she said, "Hello. Are you looking for Polly again? I don't think she's here today."

"No," he said, "actually, I came to talk to you."

"Oh," she said, surprised. She looked down at her clipboard for a moment, as if her next line would be written there, then looked up. "What about?"

"Well . . . Voodoo."

That really surprised her. She didn't look at her clipboard this time, just held it down in front of her with both hands.

"Really?" she asked. "You don't strike me as the type of man who'd believe in that."

"I'm not sure I do," he admitted, "but I do have some questions."

"Why come to me?"

"You teach history," he said. "I assume that includes local history."

"Well, that's true enough."

"And does that include Voodoo?"

"A bit."

"Then maybe you can help me."

She shrugged. "I'm willing to try. I could use a break

from taking inventory of our instruments."

"Is there someplace near here I could buy you some coffee?" he asked.

"I have a pot going in the office," she said. "How about I buy you a cup?"

"Sounds good."

"Follow me."

As they walked down a hall he asked, "Do instruments often go missing?"

"Sometimes we're missing a violin or flute at the end of the term," she said. "Turns out a student took it home and didn't bring it back."

They reached a small office with a desk, a visitor's chair and some file cabinets. On top of one of the cabinets was a coffee maker.

Karlson filled two Styrofoam cups, handed Sangster one, and then sat down behind the desk.

"Why don't you have a seat, Mr. Stark, and tell me what I can do for you?"

"Well, first you can just call me Stark," he said. "Second, I have this friend who's in sort of a coma, only the doctors don't know what's causing it."

"And you think it's Voodoo?"

"Well, Polly thinks so."

"Polly? What does she have to do with this?"

"My friend is my neighbor, Burke," Sangster said. "Polly cleans his house. And they're . . . friends."

"Friends?" Karlson said. "Oh, you mean friends."

"Right."

"I see," the teacher said. "I'm sorry to hear that her friend—your friend—is hurt."

"Well, he's not so much hurt—he did get hit on the head, but that's not the problem. He's in what the doctors are calling a coma, only it's not."

"I see."

"Is it possible for . . . something connected to

Voodoo to do that to a person?"

"There are cases of people being put into some kind of . . . coma-like state as a result of—well, let's call it a kind of post hypnotic suggestion type thing."

"So, you don't believe in Voodoo, but you do believe in hypnosis?"

"Hypnosis is a lot more believable, Stark," she said. "I mean, it's been used for years by psychiatrists to regress their patients. But the person has to be suggestible."

"So they just believe they've been hypnotized? And you're saying the same thing can be true of Voodoo."

"I'm just trying my best to give you some kind of explanation," she said.

"Okay," he said, "what would they use to induce this kind of . . . suggestible state?"

"A few things," she said. "Certain powders and charms are necessary for spells. And some knowledge of the subject, something personal, like a lock of hair or a . . . fingernail clipping . . ."

"Okay," Sangster said, "I get it. Where would I find somebody who could perform these spells?"

"Believe it or not, you can find them on the web, these days. Certain people have websites. They promise they can supply all kinds of spells—love spells, money spells, protection spells, healing spells . . ."

"Healing spell?"

"Yes."

"Okay," Sangster said, "maybe that's what I need for Burke. A healing spell."

"If you believe in that."

"I don't have to believe it do I?" he asked. "He does. Right?"

THIRTEEN

Once again Sangster took the ferry from Algiers to Canal Street. What he didn't expect was that he'd have Octavia in the car with him.

After he thanked Andrea Karlson for her help, he went back to his house to collect one of his disposable cell phones. What he found was Octavia Bourque sitting on his porch.

"Octavia," he said. "What are you doing here?"

"I came to see you." She stood up and approached him. She was dressed in the same kind of clothes she'd been wearing the night before: jeans and a tight tank top that showed off her little pokey tits.

He took a few inadvertent steps back.

"What's the matter with you?" she asked. "Don't you like girls?"

"I like . . . women very much," Sangster said. "You, you're a little girl."

"I am not a little girl." She had her hands at her sides, and closed them into fists.

"Octavia, what are you doing here?" he asked, again.

"I need a ride."

"To where?"

"The Quarter."

"Does your mom know you're going there?"

"Yes."

Sangster looked at her.

"It don't matter," she said. "She don't care. I do it all the time."

"Then why do you need a ride from me?"

"I usually walk down to the ferry. Then when I get to Canal Street I either walk or hitch a ride."

"And where do you go?"

She shrugged. "That depends."

"So where do you want to go now?"

"To that address I gave you," she said. "The Voodoo Shop."

"Why?"

"I thought I might find Isola."

"That's what I'm trying to do."

She stuck her hands in her pockets and shrugged. "So I'll help."

"Octavia—"

"I'm gonna go, whether you take me or not. Momma's really worried, and when she's worried she's a real pain in the—"

So he took her . . .

When they pulled off the ferry at Canal Street Sangster put the car in park, but left the motor running.

"Okay," he said, taking the piece of paper with the addresses on it out of his pocket. He hadn't bothered memorizing any of them. "The Voodoo shop first."

"Just drive," she said. "I'll tell you where it is."

He put the car in drive and said, "Which way?"

When Quinlan saw Sangster and the girl with the little tits he thought things might be starting to look up.

FOURTEEN

Octavia guided him to a storefront on St. Peters between Chartres and Royal. He stopped the car and turned off the engine.

"This is an art gallery," he said.

"This is the place," she said. "I'm sure of it. Octavia said she comes here all the time."

"All right," he said. "I'll check it out. You wait here."

"Stark," she said, "I can help—"

He pointed his finger at her and said, "Stay!"

"Okay!"

He got out of the car and stopped on the sidewalk to look the storefront over. There were two large windows on either side of the front door, filled with various pieces of art. The sign over the door said PAPA LEGBA'S ART GALLERY. The name was familiar. Somebody had mentioned it to him, maybe Polly, or Andrea Karlson.

He went inside.

Outside it was warm and sticky. The air-conditioning in his car was not good. He was wearing a t-shirt and jeans, the shirt sticking to his back, but as soon as he entered, the air-conditioning raised goose flesh on his arms and neck. He smelled incense in the air.

Art was represented at Papa Legba's in many different forms—paintings, drawings, sculptures, installations and more, but they all had one thing in common.

Their subject was Voodoo.

Sangster walked around the place for a few moments before someone came out of a back room. He didn't know what he'd expected, maybe somebody with dreads and a painted face. What he got was an attractive black woman with natural hair, wearing a grey suit.

"Good-afternoon," she said.

"Hello."

"Can I help you?" she asked, without any accent of any kind. "Can I help you?"

"I was just looking."

"Well," she said, "we're an art gallery, so looking is allowed. Let me know if you have any questions."

"Actually, I do have some questions, if you have the time," he said.

She looked around in an exaggerated manner and said, "I don't seem to be very busy, so yes, I have time. What would you like to know, exactly?"

"Do you know anything about healing spells?"

"Healing spells? Why would you think—why would you be interested—"

"I have a friend who's in a coma," he said, deciding to play it straight, "only it's not a coma. Do you understand?"

"You think it's a spell?"

"Don't tell me you don't believe in Voodoo," he said, spreading his arms. "With this place—"

"It's an art gallery, sir—"

"Stark," Sangster said, "my name is Stark."

"This is a gallery, Mr. Stark. We show artwork. We don't perform spells, or condone the practice of Voodoo."

"Is that right?" he asked. "Do you own this place?"

"No, I just work here."

"Are you the . . . uh, curator?"

"No. Like I said, I just work here."

"So you don't know anything about Voodoo?"

"I know enough to answer questions about the art," she said. "Look, what's going on? Who are you?"

Now it was time to lie.

"I'm looking for my niece," he said. "Her name's Isola Bourque."

"I don't know her."

"She hangs out with three other girls, and they apparently spend a lot of time here," he said. "And I don't think they're looking at art. Something else goes on here. Maybe you know about it, and maybe not."

"I don't."

"Then who does?" he asked. "Who's the curator?"

"I think you better leave, sir."

"Is he here? Maybe in the back? I just want to talk to him."

"Lloyd!" she shouted.

"Okay, yeah, that's good," he said. "Let's talk to Lloyd."

A man came out of the back room—a big black man who filled the room with his bulk. He had to duck his head to get through the doorway.

"That's Lloyd?" he asked.

"Yes," she said.

"He doesn't look like a curator."

"He's not."

"You got a problem, Kate?" Lloyd asked. His voice was a bass rumble that would have made James Earl Jones jealous.

"This gentleman was just leaving," she said. "I think he needs directions to the door."

Before Sangster could move or respond, Lloyd's big right hand landed on his shoulder. It was like being hit by a falling girder. Then the man closed his hand and the pain set in.

"This way," the big man said. "You gon' leave, you."

He walked Sangster to the door on his toes and pushed him outside.

"Okay," Sangster said, "take it easy."

"Do not come back, you," Lloyd said. Unlike Kate, he did have an accent, which sounded French. As if to confirm that fact Lloyd said, "*Passe.*"

"What?"

"He's tellin' you to go away," Octavia called, hanging out the car window.

"Oh. Look, friend, there's been a misunderstanding."

Lloyd shook his head, said "*Peeshwank*" and went back inside.

"What?" Sangster asked.

"He called you a runt," Octavia said, and then yelled, "*Peunez!*"

Sangster walked to the car.

"And what did you call him?"

"A stink bug."

"Really?"

She shrugged. "It was all I could think of."

"Where did you learn to speak French?"

"I grew up here, Stark," she said. "My mama may be Jamaican, but me, Isola and Hugo, we're all Creole."

Sangster looked back at the storefront of Papa Legba's.

"There's something else going on here," he said.

"There must be," Octavia said, "if Isola and her friends hang out here."

He leaned against the car.

"Do you know about Papa Legba?"

"Sure," she said. "He's like—"

"You can tell me on the way," Sangster said, running around to the driver's side and getting in.

"On the way where?" she asked, as he started the car.

"We're going to see your sister's girlfriends," he said.

"See if they can tell us where she is."

"They're a bunch of stuck-up bitches."

"You know them?"

"I know who they are," she said. "I've seen Isola with 'em, seen how they treat her. But she don't see it."

"She's older than you, right?"

"Three years," Octavia said, "but she's stupid."

"Octavia, whatever's gone on between you and your sister—"

"No, I mean it," she said. "My sister is dumb. She don't even know when somebody's making fun of her."

"Like these Garden District girls?"

"Right."

"Okay," he said. "That's good to know.

She fell silent. Maybe she felt badly for calling her sister names. And maybe not.

"Why don't you tell me about Papa Legba," he said.

FIFTEEN

"So Papa Legba is a Haitian Voodoo deity," Sangster said, a little while later.

"Technically," she said, "but he's also appeared in Cuba and Louisiana."

"So he's kind of an all-purpose Voodoo god."

"I guess."

The Garden District was famous for its opulent and famous historic houses surrounded with lush gardens that featured Cypress trees. However, the addresses Octavia had given Sangster for Isola's three girlfriends were not among the most expensive looking. Still, the houses were beyond anything Octavia had ever lived in, but she did her best not to look impressed.

Sangster parked in front of the first house, a two-story Colonial with two new cars in the driveway.

"Wait here," he said.

"Don't worry," Octavia said. "I don't wanna see the inside of these houses."

"I don't blame you." After all, who would want to see the inside of a home you could never live in?

He went up the walk to the front door and rang the bell. It was opened by a middle-aged woman whose face had already been stretched several times in her attempt to battle aging. She looked like a plastic doll, complete with painted on eyebrows.

"Yes?"

"Ma'am, I'm looking for Angela Grimes. Is that your daughter?"

The woman sighed, rolled her eyes and said, "Yes, what has she done now?"

"She hasn't done anything—"

"You'll have to wait for her father to get home, if you want to be reimbursed for damages—although God knows when he'll get here. I think today's the day he does mistress number one—or is it number two? I get them mixed up—"

"Mrs. Grimes, I'm not here about any damages," he said, cutting her off.

"Are you the police?"

"No."

Suddenly, she looked annoyed with him.

"Well then, I don't understand," she said. "What do you want?"

"I just want to ask your daughter some questions."

"About what?"

"About a girl named Isola Bourque."

"And who's that?"

"A friend of hers who lives in Algiers—"

"That girl?" she asked, her eyes widening. Sangster doubted any other part of her face was capable of expression. "We've told her not to associate with those people."

"Which people are those, Ma'am?" Sangster asked.

"Oh, you know," she said, "those people who live on Algiers Point."

"I live on Algiers Point," he said.

"Well, but you're obviously—I mean, . . . you're white . . . I mean, you're not . . . Creole or anything. . ." She said "Creole" like it was a dirty word.

"I see." Sangster didn't have time to deal with the woman's biased or even bigoted attitudes. "Do you know where your daughter is?"

"She's out with her friends."

"Those friends," he said, "would they be Delia

Dubois and Heather Marchand?"

"Yes," she said, "those are her friends. Why don't you try one of their houses? I don't have time—"

"I understand," Sangster said, "I don't have any more time to waste on you, either."

He turned and headed down the walk to the car. Behind him he heard the woman huff, "Well!"

"How did that go?" Octavia asked.

"Not well."

"Stuck up, right?"

He started the car and replied, "You said it."

"Yeah," Octavia said, sagely, "the mothers are probably even worse than their daughters."

After their visits to the Dubois and Marchand residences they still had no idea where the girls were. None of their mothers had any knowledge of their daughter's whereabouts, or had the time to worry about them.

"They're old enough to take care of themselves," Mrs. Marchand said.

"They're eighteen," Sangster said.

"Actually," she said, "my daughter's seventeen. But she'll be eighteen in two months."

These women should never have had children. He wondered about their fathers.

"Well," Octavia said, when he got back into the car in front of the Marchand house, "what now?"

"Now we go to the hospital and see if Burke's condition has changed."

"Will my mama be there?"

"Maybe."

"Then maybe . . ."

"She doesn't know you were coming to the Quarter today, does she?"

"Maybe not."

"So," he said, starting the engine, "you can stay in the car—again. And now, why don't you tell me the difference between Cajun and Creole."

SIXTEEN

"Okay," he said, pulling into a parking spot in the hospital lot, "so it's really more a matter of language than anything else."

"*Oui*," she said. "Both French, but different dialects."

"I get it," he said, "but we'll have to continue my education later." He got out of the car, looked at her and said, "Stay."

Octavia remained in the car while Sangster went into the hospital. If she decided to leave while he was inside, it was no skin off his nose. Even at fourteen she was old enough to get herself where she wanted to go. All the girls were. He just needed to find the Garden District girls in order to find Isola. Hopefully, she knew something about the attack on Burke. He wasn't a detective, but this all seemed pretty straightforward.

Unless Burke could tell him something that would save him some steps.

He entered the hospital through the emergency room entrance. By doing so he ran into Nurse O'Malley.

"Mr. Stark," she said, looking surprised. "What brings you back here?" She studied him. "Are you hurt?"

"No," he said, "I'm here to visit my friend."

"You're in the wrong place, then."

"I realize that," Sangster said. "It's just that I know my way around from here."

"Oh," she said, "I thought maybe it was just an excuse to see me again."

Sangster stared at her for a moment. He'd been a killer for many, many years. His flirting skills were nil.

"Nurse . . . Claire . . ."

"I'm sorry," she said, quickly. "I was just . . . of course you're concerned about your friend, and I have work to do. Nice seeing you."

Embarrassed, she put her hands in her pockets, hunched her shoulders and walked away.

Out in the parking lot Octavia sat in the passenger seat, staring out the window. She watched as doctors, nurses and patients arrived and left the hospital. A couple of ambulances also arrived and wheeled in some emergency cases.

She was bored until she saw someone else in the parking lot. Sangster didn't know, but when he went inside the Papa Legba Art Gallery she had gotten out of the car to watch through the window. That was the only reason she noticed the person walking through the parking lot. It only took a few moments for her to decide to get out of the car and follow.

When Sangster reached Burke's room there was a policeman on the door he didn't recognize.

"I'm Stark," he said.

"Yes, sir," the cop said, "go on in."

Sangster wondered why the man didn't ask for ID. He had several made out to "Stark."

When he entered the room Polly turned and looked up at him.

"How is he?"

"The same," she said. "Dere has been no change."

"He hasn't said a word," he asked, "or even opened his eyes?"

"No."

"Has the doctor been by?"

"Not since I been here."

"I'll find him, then," Sangster said. "I'd like to talk to him."

"Where is Octavia?" Polly asked.

"What?"

"Octavia," she said. "She is wit' you, isn't she?"

"Well, yes, but—"

"Don't worry," she said. "She t'ink I don't know what she's up to, but I always do."

"I see. Well, she was at my house this morning, said she wanted a ride. She said if I didn't give her a ride, she'd walk, so I just thought—"

"It is fine, Mr. Stark," Polly said. "Please don't worry. At least I know she safe with you."

"She was . . . helpful," he said. "I was trying to find those girls—"

"And did you?"

"No, not yet. I did go to the gallery, though.

"Gallery?"

"Papa Legba's Art Gallery."

"Ah . . . is that where my Isola has been goin'?"

"Supposedly," he said, "but I haven't confirmed it yet. They weren't very helpful."

"Those girls . . ."

"Yes?"

"They are not Isola's friends," she said. "I have told her that, but . . ." She shrugged.

"She didn't listen?"

"Children never do, Mr. Stark Do you have any children?"

"No," he said, "never did."

"Well, there is still time. You are a young man."

"I don't feel so young."

"Having children will not make you feel any younger."

"Then why have them?"

She gave him a pitiable look and said, "Because they are a blessin'."

"If you say so."

"Oh," she said, looking past him, "the doctor."

Sangster turned, saw the tall, gangly doctor enter the room.

"Doctor Judd."

"Mr. Stark," Judd said. "There's been no change, I'm afraid. In fact—" Judd stopped short, gave Polly a look. "Could we talk in the hall?" he asked Sangster.

"Sure."

"Excuse me," Sangster said to Polly.

She nodded, went back to Burke's bedside.

Out in the hall the doctor said, "I'm afraid if anything, his condition is worse."

"Worse in what way?" Sangster asked.

"The coma, it seems to have . . . deepened."

"I thought you said it wasn't a coma."

Judd shrugged his bony shoulders and said, "We don't know what else to call it. In any case, he seems to have gone . . . deeper into it."

"There's nothing you can do to bring him out of it? Even for a few moments?"

"The police asked the same thing," Judd said, "and the answer is, no. Since we don't know what's causing it, we can't counteract it, even for a minute."

"Doctor," Sangster said, "what do you know about Voodoo?"

"Voodoo?" Judd looked startled. "Just what everyone else knows, I suppose. Dolls, Zombies . . . why? Oh wait, you're not about to suggest that this is some sort of . . . Voodoo spell?"

"In all your time as a doctor here in New Orleans,

have you ever had a case of someone . . . affected by Voodoo?"

"Well one or two, but it usually turns out to be someone high on PCP or ecstasy who thinks they've been cursed. I mean . . . there's no such thing as Voodoo, Mr. Sangster." An announcement came over the PA system and Judd said, "I'm sorry, that's me."

"Of course."

Sangster turned to watch the doctor go, and saw Octavia coming toward him.

"What are you doing here?" he asked. "I thought you were going to stay in the car. Your mother's in Burke's room."

"I know," she said, "I just thought you should know . . ."

"Know what?"

". . . I saw someone in the parking lot, somebody from that gallery?"

"What? What were they doing?"

"Just walking, but—"

"What did you do?"

"I followed them."

"And?"

"They came into the hospital and talked to somebody."

"Who did they talk to?"

She pointed in the direction Dr. Judd had just gone and said, "That man."

"Dr. Judd?"

"I don't know his name, but it was him."

"That's Burke's doctor."

"Then you should be glad I came in and told you."

"Okay," he said, "you keep saying 'they.' Who did you see? Was it Lloyd, the big man you called a stink bug?"

"No," she said, smugly, "it was the lady."

"Yep. The lady from the gallery?"

"The pretty lady in the suit."

"Kate," he said. "That was her name."

"Who was she?"

"She said she was just a clerk," he said, "but I'm starting to think she was a lot more than that."

SEVENTEEN

Sangster walked through the hospital to see if he could spot Kate anywhere, taking Octavia with him.

"Just to give you a heads up," he said, "your mom knows you're with me."

"You told her?"

"Not me," he said. "She already knew."

"That Hugo," she said, "he got a big mouth on him. She mad?"

"Didn't seem to be."

"What'd you tell 'er?"

"That you were helping me."

"Maybe that's why she ain't mad."

"Maybe."

They checked the entire floor, then went down to the first. Sangster found himself in the emergency room section once again.

"Which way did she come in?" he asked Octavia.

"This way."

"How close behind her were you?"

"Not far."

"Did you see her when you came in?"

"No," Octavia said, "so I asked where your friend's room was."

"You remembered his name?"

"Sure," she said. "Mama's always sayin' 'I'm goin' to clean Burke's house'."

"Did you see her on that floor?"

"No."

"Okay," he said, "why don't you go back out to the car. I'll be out in a little while."

"Sure. I'll only come back in if I see Papa Legba himself." She said it with a grin.

"You do that."

She went out. He turned, found himself facing Nurse O'Malley, again.

"Oh," she said, "hi."

"Hello."

They both felt awkward.

"Nurse O'Malley—"

"Claire," she said, "please. If we're going to keep running into each other . . ."

"Claire, then," he said. "Have you seen an attractive black woman wearing a grey suit in the hospital during the last fifteen minutes?"

"No one like that down here," she said.

"She came in this door."

"Then she must have gotten by me," she said. "I can ask around."

"I'd appreciate it," he said. "I'll be on the second floor for a few more minutes, then I'll come down here to leave by this door."

"I'll see what I can find out for you."

"Thank you."

"Are you working with the police?" she asked.

"No," he said, "but we're not working against each other."

He went back upstairs, where Polly was still at Burke's bedside. As Sangster entered she released the old man's hand.

"You're back," she said.

"I spoke with the doctor," he said. "Burke's coma— for want of a better word—has deepened."

She stood up to face him and folded her arms.

"So what will you do now?"

"Have you seen a woman in the hospital?" he asked. "Black, well-dressed, in the last fifteen, twenty minutes?"

"No."

"Has anyone else been by to see Burke since you've been here?"

"No."

The woman had come into the hospital to see someone. What he didn't know was if it was a patient? Or someone who worked here? Was it just coincidence, or did it have to do with Burke? And if it concerned Burke, did it have something to do with Voodoo?

Her name was Kate, but he didn't know her last name. And he didn't know Lloyd's last name. Maybe he should find out.

"Guess I'm going back to Algiers. Do you want a ride?"

"No," she said, "I'll stay until they kick me out. I borrowed a friend's car. Besides, you do not want me and my Octavia in de car at de same time. Trust me." She said it with a smile.

"All right," he said. He started to leave, then turned back. "Look, all I know about Voodoo is Marie Laveau, and that's only because I've lived here a few years."

"Marie is a Voodoo Queen," Polly said. "She's the most powerful figure in Louisiana Voodoo. Dr. John was a Voodoo King. Some say he is even the power behind Marie."

Sangster noticed that all Polly's references to the Voodoo Queen and King were present tense.

"What about Papa Legba?" he asked. "Where does he fit in? Octavia told me a little bit."

"She only know a little bit," Polly said. "Papa Legba stands at the crossroads. He gives permission for mortals to communicate with the loa. The loa are spirits."

"Is he a King, then?"

"He himself is a loa," she said. "A spirit."

"Why would someone named their art gallery after him?" he asked.

"Perhaps it is to honor him," she said. "Or, to attract the tourists?" She shrugged. "There is also a Marie Laveau House of Voodoo in the Vieux Carre."

"And what is it, exactly?" he asked.

She smiled. "A gift shop."

Before heading back to Algiers Sangster wanted to make one more stop. He parked at the corner of St. Ann and Chartres Streets, then they walked along Chartres into Jackson Square, past the St. Louis Cathedral until they reached Pirates Alley.

Sangster didn't know from which direction Burkes had entered the Alley, from Royal or the way he and Octavia had just done. But according to Telemaco, Burke had been found lying here, alongside the garden of the Cathedral.

"Is this the place?" Octavia asked.

"This is it?"

She looked over at the Pirates Alley Café and sad, "That's cute. Can we have something?"

"No," he said, "we're not here to eat."

Next to the café was the Faulkner Bookstore, situated in a building where William Faulkner had lived while he wrote his first novel, SOLDIER'S PAY. Sangster had spent much time in that bookstore in the past, but they were also not there to buy books.

"So what do you see?" she asked.

"Nothing," he said, staring at the cobblestoned street. "Nothing at all."

"Maybe the police found something," she said.

"Maybe."

"What do you think he was doin' here?"

"All I can think was that he was meeting somebody."

"And somebody hit him either before or after?"

"No," he said, looking at her, "nobody intended to meet him, at all. He was sent here to be attacked."

"By who?"

Sangster shook his head. "That's what this is all about, isn't it?"

EIGHTEEN

Sangster drove back to Algiers, dropped Octavia at her house.

"Your mama said Hugo's with a neighbor," he told her.

"I know who," she said. "I'll fetch him."

"Octavia," he said, "try and stay close to home until I can locate your sister, okay?"

"But I can help."

"It would be a help to me if I don't have to worry about you while I'm looking," he explained. "Stay close to home, watch your brother."

"You think me and my brother are in danger?"

"Well, your sister's nowhere to be found. Burke went looking for her and ended up in the hospital. What do you think?"

"I think me and Hugo would be safer with you."

Sangster opened his mouth to reply, but it occurred to him then that she might be right. But he couldn't very well move around with Octavia and Hugo hanging on his coattails.

"I'm going to think about that, Octavia," he said. "For now, just go get your brother and stay close to home."

"What about my mama?" Octavia asked. "Do you think she's in danger?"

"I'm sure your mama will be all right," he said. "Now get your brother and I'll be in touch."

He remained there, watching from the car while Octavia went next door, got her brother, and took him into the house, leading him by the ear. He figured the boy was going to get it when they got inside.

He started the car and drove away.

When he got home he realized he hadn't eaten all day and was hungry. Leaving the car parked in front of his house, he walked to the Old Point Bar.

It was still early enough for the live music to be going on. The Bottoms Up Blues Gang, an acoustic trio consisting of a female singer, a male guitar player and a male harmonica player, was on stage. There was also a juke box at the Point, so Sangster chose to take a table outside on the sidewalk, where he ordered some tacos and Tin Roof beer.

He was working on a second beer when he noticed, man walking up the street toward him. It was dark, but as the figure came into the lights he saw that it was Father Patrick. The priest was once again without his collar, and was carrying something under his arm.

As he reached Sangster's table he said, "I was hoping I'd find you here again tonight."

"You're lucky," Sangster said. "I just happened to be hungry. What have you got there?"

Father Patrick took the item out and said, "A chess set. Interested?"

"Set 'em up," Sangster said.

By this time they were the only ones seated outside. While Father Patrick set up the pieces of the simple plastic Staunton chess set, Sangster ordered another plate of tacos, and two more Tin Roofs.

Father Patrick arranged it so white was on Sangster's side. The first move was his.

"How was your day?" the priest asked.

"Uneventful."

"Still looking into the meaning of a soul? Or Voodoo?"

"Both."

"Anything you want to talk about?"

Sangster thought about asking the priest more about his soul, but this wasn't the place to have such a discussion. Instead, he filled him in about Burke, and what had happened to the old guy. Even without his collar the priest seemed like a man he could talk to, and other than Burke, he didn't have any friends. Burke knew about Sangster's past as a hitman, and how he had awakened one morning to find that he had a soul, and so had given up being a killer. But he didn't replay any of that for Father Patrick.

"It sounds like your friend needs a miracle," Father Patrick said.

"Give me a break, Father," Sangster said. "I have enough trouble dealing with souls and Voodoo, don't let's go throwing miracles into the mix."

They played four games of chess, of which Father Patrick won three.

"You're very good," the priest said, as they set the pieces up for a fifth game.

"Apparently, not as good as you, but I'm missing my regular partner. We're a little more evenly matched."

"Burke?"

Sangster nodded.

"Well, he'll be out of the hospital eventually, won't he?" Father Patrick asked.

"I'm not so sure," Sangster said.

"You're not thinking that it really is Voodoo, are you?"

"I have it on good authority that if you believe something, you can make it happen."

"Like a Voodoo spell?"

Sangster nodded.

"But that also sounds like it would be true of a . . ." He trailed off.

"Miracle?" Sangster asked.

"I didn't say it."

"You almost did."

"So what do you plan to do?"

"Tomorrow I'll start looking again."

"For whoever hurt your friend?" the priest asked." Isn't that the police's job?"

"Maybe it is," Sangster said, "but Polly has asked me to find her daughter."

"Do you think she's been hurt, too?"

"I hope not," Sangster said. "If someone has hurt Burke and her, then what about the rest of Polly's family?"

"How many more?"

"Two more children, a little boy and another teenage girl."

"Do you really think they're in danger?"

"It's possible. If I knew someone, I'd ask," Sangster said.

"What are you, anyway?" Father Patrick asked. "A detective? An ex-cop? Maybe a mercenary of some kind?"

"None of those things," Sangster said. "I'm just someone who can help—if I have the time, and a free hand."

"You mean if you don't have to worry about Polly and her kids," Patrick said.

"Yes. Checkmate."

"Good game," Patrick said, sitting back. "Why don't I do it?"

"Do what?" Sangster asked.

"Protect them."

"But . . . you're a priest."

"So what? I'm still a man. I can stay with them until you've done what you have to do. Or better yet, bring them to the church. I'll give them sanctuary."

Sangster thought as moment, then said, "Now that last part might not be a bad idea."

Quinlan watched as Sangster and the other man played game after game of chess. He had the feeling that this was not part of any routine he'd seen Sangster indulge in over the past couple of days. Something was going on.

Quinlan decided to go back to his French Quarter B&B and plan his move.

NINETEEN

The next morning Sangster took Polly, Octavia and Hugo to the church.

"Oh, man," Octavia said, "I gotta go into a church?"

"It's either that or a police station," Sangster lied.

"Police station!" Hugo voted.

"Never mind," Polly said. "Mr. Stark is doin' what he t'ink is best for us."

"Nobody expects you to convert, Octavia," he said to the teenager.

Sangster had arrived at their house early in the morning, hoping to catch Polly before she went to work. It took him a few moments of conversation on her porch to convince the woman that the idea was a sound one.

"I still got to go to work," she said, "but I would feel better knowin' my children were safe."

Sangster argued against her going to work, but she said she couldn't afford to lose any of the jobs she had.

"Then be very careful about strangers," he said.

"I am always careful," she said. "A woman alone got to be."

He took them not to the church, but to the front door of the rectory. Since he was expecting them, Father Patrick answered the door himself.

"Welcome," he said, "to the Holy Name of St. Mary."

"Father Patrick," Sangster said, "meet Polly and her two kids, Octavia and Hugo."

To her credit Octavia suddenly looked self-conscious in her cut off shorts and tank top. Both she and Hugo had backpacks with some extra clothes. Sangster was carrying a small suitcase for Polly.

A middle-aged woman appeared behind Father Patrick.

"This is our housekeeper, Mrs. Cox," he introduced. "She'll show you to your rooms."

"This way, folks," the woman said, pleasantly. She put a welcoming hand on Hugo's shoulder. Octavia threw a worried glance at Sangster over her shoulder as they all left the room.

"You still sure you want to do this, Patrick?" Sangster asked.

"It'd be a little late for me to change my mind now, Stark," the priest said. "It's fine. Mrs. Cox will take good care of them."

"And your Monsignor?"

"I convinced him that Polly was seeking sanctuary from an abusive spouse, and that it would only be for a few days. He actually has to leave town for a few days, so he wasn't too concerned."

"Okay, good. Are there any other entrances or exits to the building?"

"A back door, always kept locked."

Sangster knew no lock would stop someone who was determined to get in.

"You better tell Mrs. Cox she should keep an eye on Octavia. I wouldn't put it past her to sneak out."

"I'll tell her. You think maybe we can get that young girl to wear a bra while she's here?"

"That's between you and her," Stark said, raising his hands, "or Mrs. Cox and her."

"And the boy?"

"Well, he voted to go to a police station," Sangster said, "so maybe the sheer size of the church, and all the statues, might impress him."

"I'll tell him some Bible stories," Patrick said.

"Maybe that'll do it."

"Do you believe everything in the Bible yourself?" Sangster asked.

"That doesn't matter," Patrick said, "they're good stories, like Hercules movies."

Sangster remembered how much he'd liked Hercules movies when he was a kid. He'd never equated them to stories in the Bible, but thinking about David and Goliath, Noah's Ark and the Ten Commandments, he figured Father Patrick was probably right.

"Okay, then," he said, "I'll wait outside for Polly. She insists on going to work, so I'll drive her."

"I'll see you later, then," Patrick said. "I can still get you at the cell number you gave me last night, right?"

"Right."

Patrick nodded, slapped Sangster on the back as he went out the front door.

Sangster waited in the car for Polly to reappear. When she got in the car she was quiet.

"Everything okay?" he asked.

"No," she said, putting her hand to her head. "When I asked Burke to help me, I never expected all . . . all this."

"No point in beating yourself up about it now, Polly," Sangster said. "We gotta do what we gotta do."

She looked at him. "And now I drag you into it."

"Whoa," Sangster said, "I dragged myself into it. I like Burke, and I don't like the idea of somebody putting him in the hospital and getting away with it."

"You gon' kill 'em when you find' em?"

Sangster frowned, considered his answer for a moment.

"What did Burke tell you about me?"

"Nothin'," she said. "He just say you his neighbor,

he like you, and you keep to yourself. Oh, he said you a shit chess player." She grinned.

"He said that?"

"I t'ink he was kiddin'."

"He better be. No, I'm not going to kill anybody, Polly. Why would you ask that?"

"I don't know." She shrugged. "You mind if I say what I t'ink?"

"No, I don't mind," he said. "In fact, I'd prefer it."

"I t'ink maybe you a dangerous man, Stark."

"And how do you feel about that?"

"I t'ink me and my kids, maybe dat's what we need, right now."

TWENTY

Polly was cleaning one of the other Algiers Point schools that day. Considering how easily he'd gotten into Edna Karr High, Sangster hoped she'd be safe there.

He said he'd see her at the church later in the evening, and drove from there to the ferry. He drove to St. Peters and Chartres Streets, this time parking on Chartres. He walked down St. Peters until he came to the Papa Legba Art Gallery. He peered in the window, wondering if Kate was working that day, and whether or not Lloyd was there, as well. He stared through the window until he saw Kate come out of the back room. It was now obvious that she was working, but he still didn't know about Lloyd. He decided to take the chance. Maybe the big man was off having breakfast somewhere.

When he walked in, Kate started to smile, but it died on her face when she saw him.

"You!"

"Me."

"What do you want?"

"Just to talk."

"You should leave."

"Or what? You'll call Lloyd?"

"That's right."

"I think if Lloyd was here you'd have called him by now," he said.

He could tell by her eyes that he was right. But he didn't know how long he had before Lloyd would show up.

"You lied to me yesterday."

"Did I?" she asked. "About what?"

There was a pleasant, musky smell in the air. He moved a step closer, and realized it was coming from her. He took another step, and she held her ground.

"You're much more than just a clerk around here," he said. "Am I right?"

"Perhaps." She was wearing another suit, but this one was blue. Her hair was still natural, her lipstick blood red, with earrings to match. A chain hung around her neck, but whatever was at the end of it was hidden, nestled in her deep cleavage, which was visible because the top two buttons of her white shirt were undone. "But still not the curator, I'm afraid."

"Second in command, then."

She smiled. "Of this place? You make it sound so . . . grandiose."

"Look," he said, "I just have some questions. Would it hurt you to answer them?"

She took a deep breath, regarded him for a moment, then said, "Would you like some tea?"

"Tea? Sure, tea would be fine."

"Come with me."

She turned and led him into the back room, which was much larger than he would have thought, and furnished like a lavish living room.

"Make yourself comfortable."

Sangster sat. "More and more the Papa Legba Gallery is less and less what I expected."

"And what did you expect?" she asked. "Dolls? Altars? Sacrifices?"

"I don't know," he said. "Incense, at least."

She turned with a smile, holding a tray with a pot and two cups on it.

"I hate incense," she said, setting the tray down on the coffee table in front of him. "Shall I serve?"

"Sure."

"Milk or sugar?"

"Just straight."

She poured him a cup of tea, then one for herself, to which she added two spoons of sugar. Then she sat across from him.

"Did you tell me your name?"

He didn't bother answering the question, just said, "Stark."

"Well, Mr. Stark," she said, crossing her fine legs, "you mentioned some questions?"

"Yes, I did," he said. "I'm looking for a girl who is supposed to have spent time here with some friends of hers. Her name is Isola Bourque. She's hanging around with three girls from the Garden District."

"And where is Miss Isola from?" Kate asked.

"Algiers."

"Ah . . ."

"What's wrong with Algiers? I live there."

"Nothing is wrong with it," she said. "I just wondered why three Garden girls were hanging around with a girl who . . . well, obviously wasn't from the Garden District."

"So they were here?"

"They've been here a time or two."

"And?"

She shrugged. "They were interested in Voodoo. For some reason they thought this was the place to come to learn about it."

"Why did they think that? Did they say?"

"One said somebody told her that," Kate said. "I don't know who it was."

"And what did you tell them?"

"That they came to the wrong place. That was the first time they came."

"And the second?"

"I told them the same thing," she said.

"Did they listen?"

"No."

"What did you say then?"

"I recommended some other places they might go."

"Can you give me the same names?"

"Sure. I'll write them down for you."

She stood up, walked to a desk, grabbed a pad of paper and started writing.

"Are all the places here in the Quarter?" Sangster asked.

She tore a page from the pad, turned to face him.

"I only gave them a few places, and made sure they were around here. I didn't want to get into trouble for sending teenage girls out into the bayou."

"Why there?"

She handed him the slip of paper. "It's said that Marie II, Marie Laveau's daughter, performed public rituals out there. If I was really going to send someone to find out about Voodoo, that's where I'd send them."

"Where in the bayou, exactly?"

"Oh, I don't know. Bayou Teche, Bayou St. John, someplace like that."

"I see." He looked at the paper in his hand. On it she had written *Marie Laveau's House of Voodoo, Rev. Zombie's Voodoo Shop*, and the *New Orleans Historic Voodoo Museum*.

He stood up and said, "Well, you've been very helpful. I'll try not to bother you again."

"I hope you find the girl you're looking for."

She walked him back around to the shop, and watched him go out the door.

He walked to his car wondering why she had been very helpful, this time.

TWENTY-ONE

He drove to the third address on the list. The New Orleans Historic Voodoo Museum was on Dumaine Street, between Bourbon and Royal. It collected all the history, rituals and folklore of Voodoo and was in the heart of the French Quarter. Included was the story of Marie Laveau, and a walking tour to St. Louis Cemetery #1, where her crypt was.

Sangster paid his seven dollar entry fee, walked around a bit, eventually made his way to the gift shop which sold, among other things, Voodoo dolls, gris-gris bags, ritual candles and books. Maybe this was, indeed, the place some teenage girls would come to learn about the subject.

It still bothered Sangster that Kate had been so helpful at the Papa Legba when the first time he was there she'd had him escorted out by big Lloyd. What had changed her attitude? Did it have anything to do with her visit to the hospital? He still had no idea who'd she'd been there to visit, or talk to.

He took a paperback book about Auntie Laveau—THE VOODOO QUEEN by Robert Tallant—off a shelf and carried it to the thirtyish cashier.

"Did you find what you wanted?" she asked.

"Pretty much," he said, handing her a twenty dollar bill. "I was actually looking for the daughter of a friend of mine. She comes here a lot."

"Oh?" the woman asked, giving him his change.

"Yes, she and her friends—there'd be four of them all together. Three white girls and a light-skinned black girl. Have you seen them?"

"Probably."

"What do you mean, probably?"

"I mean, I'm here most days, so if they were here I probably saw them, but I don't remember. I see so many people."

"Well, they're very interested in Voodoo. They might have bought something, like a doll, or a . . . what do you call it . . . the bag?"

"Gris-Gris bag?"

"Yes."

"Well they would have had to buy it from me."

"This girl, she would have been very pretty young—"

"Mister, I see a lot of pretty girls. This is New Orleans. They're all pretty and young." She said the last part almost bitterly. She looked past him and asked the next customer, "Did you find what you wanted?"

Sangster stepped aside. He looked around. There were families with kids, teenagers on their own, mostly tourists. It made sense that somebody might not remember a bunch of teenage girls.

Maybe he'd have better luck at the other two places.

He left the museum. When he got back to his car there was a man leaning against his door, eating a Lucky Dog he had to have gotten from a vendor in nearby Jackson Square.

"Hey, Sangster," he said, which concerned Sangster because nobody in New Orleans knew that name.

Quinlan had decide how and when to make his move.

He once again followed Sangster when he left Algiers, tailed him to the Papa Legba Gallery and then here to the Voodoo Museum. And this was where he decided to make contact. As Sangster went into the museum,

Quinlan got himself a couple of Lucky Dogs from a street vendor and leaned against the car to wait.

"What's your name?" Sangster asked.

"Quinlan."

Sangster didn't know it, but that didn't mean anything. The man could have gotten into the business after he left it.

Quinlan was tall, whipcord thin, in his early thirties. He stood with an easy confidence that was not in the least arrogant. The lack of arrogance was what would make him dangerous.

"Who sent you?" Sangster asked.

"Nobody," Quinlan said. "I came on my own."

"How'd you find me?"

"That's for me to know."

"I'm not carrying," Sangster said.

"That makes two of us," Quinlan said. "This is just—well, a sort of hello."

It was probably more of a scouting mission, to feel him out, see how much he'd lost.

"Wait," he said. "You were in my house, weren't you?"

"Now, there you go," Quinlan said. "You never spotted me following you these last few days, so I was thinking maybe you'd lost it. But now that makes me feel better."

"About what?"

"About killing you." Quinlan finished his dog and crumpled the paper into a ball. He pushed off the car and stood straight. "Eventually."

"What do you want?" Sangster asked.

"What do any of us want?" Quinlan asked. "I want to be the best. For that to happen. I have to beat the best. Ain't that what Ric Flair always said? 'To be the man, you got to beat the man.' You're the man, Sangster."

"Maybe I was, once," Sangster said. "Not anymore."

"Oh," Quinlan said, "that kind of a reputation doesn't just go away. Especially not after . . . Las Vegas?"

Sangster flipped the paper bag holding the Marie Laveau book through the rear window onto the seat of the car.

"What do you think you know about Las Vegas?"

"I know you killed people there," Quinlan said. "A bunch of people. Professionals. Including your old handler, Primble."

Sangster stared at the man, who seemed so sure of his facts there didn't seem to be any point in denying anything.

"So, what do you need, Quinlan?"

"I'm just . . . feeling you out. Haven't you ever done that with a mark?"

"No," Sangster said, "I haven't. I never got to know a mark."

"Well, to tell you the truth, neither have I," Quinlan said. "This just seemed like a special case."

"You don't want to take me on, Quinlan."

"Why not?" Quinlan asked. "You just told me you're not the man, anymore."

"Just because I'm out of the business doesn't mean I'll stand still and let you kill me."

"I wouldn't expect you to. But to stop me, Sangster, you'd have to see me coming. And you won't." Quinlan tossed the balled up hot dog wrapper into the car, where it landed on the back seat next to the bag. "Get rid of that for me, won't you?"

He turned and walked away.

TWENTY-TWO

Another time, another place, Quinlan wouldn't have gotten off that street alive. But this wasn't another time, when Sangster's only reaction to a threat would have been violence. He was going to have to give this man, Quinlan, some serious thought, maybe make a call or two to find out who he really was. But for now he decided to stick to his schedule, which meant checking out both Marie Laveau's House of Voodoo and Rev. Zombie's Voodoo Shop.

As it turned out, Marie Laveau's and Reverend Zombie's were, for all intents and purposes, one and the same. They shared a storefront on St. Peters Street off of Bourbon. It was a full service Voodoo shop, which meant they would teach you how to cast a spell, and sell you what you needed to do it. They sold talismans, charms, tribal masks, statues, dolls, things called ritual bags, offering bags, mojo bags, and actual spell kits.

The guy behind the counter was an old black man with dreads stuffed beneath a bulging cloth cap and ashy skin, the whites of his eyes more yellow than anything else. When he smiled his mouth gleamed with gold.

"How kin me help you, mon?"

The man was distinctly Jamaican, so Sangster said, "I'm assuming that most or all of this stuff represents Haitian Voodoo?"

"You know anyt'in' about Voodoo, mon?" the man asked.

"I know there are different kinds," Sangster said. "Haitian, Louisiana, African . . ."

"Den you know more den mos' folks," the man said, "but lemme tell you one thing, mon." He leaned forward, as if to give his words more import. "Voodoo is Voodoo, mon. An' you can use what you buy here for any kind of Voodoo spell."

"I see."

The man leaned back.

"And do you sell to anyone?"

"Anyone."

"You must get a lot of tourists in here wanting to learn how to cast spells."

"Jus' between you and me, mon," the clerk said, "tourists just wan' look."

"But you do get people in here who want to learn?"

"Oh, yes," he said, "we get dem, an' we get de real *houngans* and *mambos*, mon, both new and experienced. Dey the male and female priests who really know dere stuff. Dis is de place to come and get whatchoo need if you want to make *gris-gris*." It was pronounced "gree-gree."

"What's your name?"

"My name Malik," the man said, with a big grin.

"I'm Stark."

"Well, Mr. Stark—"

"Not Mister," Sangster said, "just Stark."

"Stark," Malik said, "are you a police-man?"

"No," Sangster said. "I'm looking for some teenage girls. I think they're wanting to learn Voodoo."

"You not lookin' for tourists, mon?"

"No," Sangster said, "they live here. Three of them live in the Garden District, one in Algiers. She's a Creole girl, interested in her heritage."

"Lots of Creole gals in the Veax Carre, mon."

"That's true," Sangster said. "This one is seventeen, light-skinned, pretty, built kind of . . ." He trailed off. He was actually describing Octavia, assuming that Isola would just be a slightly older version.

"I t'ink I gotchoo, man," the clerk said, with a grin. "Dem Creole gals, dey real sexy, even dat young."

"She's the daughter of a friend," Sangster said. "And she probably would have been asking a lot of questions."

"You know," Malik said, "I t'ink maybe I know who you mean. Coupla days ago a gal come in here, real curious about spells. She ask a lot of questions, and I t'ink dey was some girls waitin' outside for her."

"What did she buy? Did she say anything about where she was going?"

"She buy some t'ings," Malik said, "maybe some mojo bags, me not so sure. She have dem little titties, you know?" Malik wriggled his eyebrows. "Wit dem nipples, whatchoo call . . . pokies? Me have trouble lookin' at anyt'ing else."

"Yeah, okay," Sangster said. "Did she say anything about why she was buying those things?"

"Well, she ask some questions about spells, but me don't mess wit' that stuff, mon. Me no *houngan*, me just sell the stuff."

"Then who did she ask?"

"Sharise."

"Who's Sharise?"

"She works here," Malik said. "She supposed to be a *Mambo*."

"Supposed to be?"

"She advertised as a *Mambo* who can teach spells."

"But is she?"

"To believe she is Voodoo priestess you must first believe in Voodoo," Malik said.

"Okay, never mind," Sangster said. "Whether she is or isn't, can I talk to her?"

"Sure."

"Where is she?"

"Not here."

"Is she coming in?"

"Tomorrow morning."

"Can you tell me where she lives?"

"Me could tell you dat, mon," Malik said, "but den I get fired."

"You don't own this place?"

"Me?" Malik laughed.

"Then does Sharise?"

"No, she just work here, like me."

"Then who owns it?"

Malik shrugged, "Dat be a mystery."

"Are you kidding?"

"Look," Malik said, "you wanna talk to Sharise, you come back tomorrow. I can't tell you more den dat, mon. Sorry."

Sangster frowned. Again, he was stuck between the old and the new. In the old days he would have wrung the information out of the clerk. Maybe now he could buy it. Not that he had a lot of money, but maybe a twenty would do. He took it out of his pocket.

"Unless you lookin' to buy a spell bag, you better put dat away, mon," Malik said. "Come back tomorrow. Sharise will talk to you."

"Okay," Sangster said, stuffing the bill back into his pocket. He started for the door, but was struck by a thought that made him turn back.

"Can I ask you one more thing?"

"Go ahead."

"Do you know the people who work over at the Papa Legba Gallery?"

"I know dem."

"And Kate?"

"Kate Bouchard."

"She works there, right?"

Malik smiled broadly, happily exposing most of his gold teeth.

"She do more den work dere, mon."

"That's not what she told me."

"Den she pullin' your leg," Malik said, with a laugh. "She own de place."

"Thanks, Malik."

"Hey, mon."

Sangster turned back.

"Dat information may be worth twenty dollars to you?" he asked.

"No, mon," Sangster said, and walked out.

TWENTY-THREE

From Marie Laveau's, Sangster went back to Algiers. He had a lot to think about, not the least of which was the appearance in his life of Quinlan. Sangster realized that being out of the murder business did not mean he should lose his edge. He had not spotted Quinlan on his tail, and who knew how long it had taken him to realize that somebody—no doubt Quinlan—had been in his house?

He decided to go home first before going to the church to check on Polly and her kids. Hopefully, Quinlan had not been watching him when he left them in Father Patrick's care. He might perceive them as Sangster's weakness.

He parked Burke's car in front of the old man's house and walked over to his. As he approached the porch he realized someone was there, sitting. He hoped it wasn't Octavia again, but he would have preferred her to Quinlan. As it turned out, it was neither of them.

"I've been wonderin' when you'd get home," Detective Telemaco said. "Sorry to surprise you."

"Is your partner with you?"

"No."

"Then don't worry about it."

"You want to come inside?"

"Not necessarily," Telemaco said. "We can talk out here."

"Want a beer?"

"Sure."

Sangster went inside, grabbed two Blackened

Voodoos from the fridge—the irony did not escape him—and went back outside. He handed Telemaco one of the cool, sweaty bottles and sat across from him. The table between them was empty. Usually, it had a chess board set up on it for a game with Burke.

"Is this about Burke?" he asked. "Is something wrong?"

"Not that I know of," Telemaco said. "Last time I heard, there was no change."

"So what's this about?"

Telemaco hesitated, sipped from his bottle, then said, "We found a dead girl. A teenager."

"Where?"

"Jackson Square—in the park."

Isola? he thought.

"Who was she?"

"Her name was Angela Grimes."

"Shit."

"Did you know her?"

"No," Sangster said, "but the girl I'm looking for did."

"We talked to her parents," Telamaco said. "The mother said a man fitting your description came by to talk to her about her daughter."

"Yeah," Sangster said, "only she didn't have time for me, just like she never has time for her daughter."

"And the other girls? Are their parents the same?"

"Yeah," Sangster said. "The Dubois and Marchand families are apparently very similar."

"So ya'll figure these girls are out there somewhere with Creole girl? Polly's daughter?"

"Isola," Sangster said, "yes. Tell me, how was the girl killed?"

"Strangled," Telemaco said. "Nothing Voodoo about it."

"But they're interested in Voodoo," Sangster said. "I

tracked Octavia to Marie Laveau's, and maybe to the Papa Legba Gallery."

"They say they saw her?"

"Fella named Malik at Marie Laveau's says maybe," Sangster said. "I was planning to go back there tomorrow to talk to a lady named Sharise. She might know something."

"Planning?"

"So," Sangster said, "here comes the part where you warn me off. It's your case."

"I'm working a murder," Telemaco said, "not a missing persons case. And none of the families have reported their girls missing."

"Well, they might," Sangster said, "now that the Grimes girl is dead."

"Maybe," Telemaco said, "but I don't have any objection to ya'll still looking for your girl. Ya'll's friend Polly's daughter. Hell, ya'll might find out something interesting."

"If I do, I'll pass it on to you, Detective."

"That's all I ask." The detective finished his beer and set it down on the table. "Thanks for your time." He got up and started down the walk.

Sangster stood up and walked to the top of the steps. "Detective!"

"Yo!" Telemaco turned around.

"You've never been here before. How did you know where I lived?" The ID Sangster had shown the man when they first met did not have this address on it.

Telemaco laughed.

"I've known where you live since before you went to Vegas last year, Stark." He waved and walked to his car, which was parked down the street.

TWENTY-FOUR

Sangster got himself a beer, carried it out to the porch along with one of his disposable cell phones. He took a long swig, then dialed the number for Mickey Grey in Brooklyn, Illinois, where he ran a strip club that was much more than a strip club.

"Hello?" a voice answered.

"Do you know who this is?"

"I do if you're still alive, man," Mickey Grey said. "I heard about Vegas."

"I'd prefer not to talk about that."

"Okay," Mickey said. "What can I do for you? You in town?"

"No, I'm not," Sangster said. "I need you to look into somebody for me. That is, unless you already know about him."

Mickey was a fifty-one-year-old black man, but over the phone he sounded like a white stock broker.

"I'll give it my best shot," he said.

"Quinlan."

Mickey was quiet.

"You know him?"

"I know him," Mickey said.

"What's his rep?"

"He's bad," Mickey said, "because he's so good."

"How good?"

"Good enough that you don't want to go up against him if you're, say, out of practice?"

Sangster didn't respond.

"Have you seen him," Mickey asked, "or just heard about him?"

"Oh, I've seen him."

"Then you've got trouble."

"That's what I wanted to know."

"Do you need help?"

To get help from Mickey would mean telling him where he was. That was just as likely to bring more trouble as it was help.

"No," he said, "I'll handle it."

"Well, if you're sure," Mickey said. "If you change your mind, you know where I am."

"I know," Sangster said. "Thanks, Mickey."

Sangster knocked on the rectory door and waited. The housekeeper, Mrs. Cox, answered it.

"Mrs. Cox," Sangster said. "I'm Stark—"

"I remember you. They're in the church."

"Is everything okay?" he asked.

"Everythin' fine, young man," Mrs. Cox said. "Those children are delightful. The boy is smart as a whip, and the girl showed me how to make gumbo the right way." She shook her head. "I always thought I already knew how. I still got some left, if you're hungry."

"That sounds fine, Ma'am," he said. "I'll just go and tell them I'm here."

"I'll have it waitin' for you when you come in."

"Thank you."

She closed the door. He went back up the walk, then next door to the church. When he entered he heard voices, saw Father Patrick at the front of the center aisle with Polly, Octavia and Hugo. He wasn't sure whether Polly would be there or at the hospital. In that moment he felt kind of bad that he hadn't gone to see Burke before returning home.

He walked down the aisle toward them, saw that Patrick was telling them about the stained-glass window above the altar. They all turned to face him when they heard his footsteps.

"Stark!" Octavia said. "It's about time."

"Nice to be appreciated." He looked at Patrick, who was now wearing his collar and cassock. "How'd things go today?"

"Pretty quietly," Patrick said. "We spent most of the day in the rectory. When it got dark I thought I'd give them a tour of the church.

Octavia gave Sangster a look that said, "Save me."

"Mrs. Cox tells me you showed her how to make proper gumbo," Sangster said. "I think I'd like to sample some of that myself."

"I'll go in and get it ready for you," she offered.

"'Tavia," her mother said, "Father ain't done yet—"

"It's all right, Polly," Father Patrick said. "I get the feeling Stark has some things to talk to us about."

"I do need to talk to Polly and Octavia," Sangster said. He gave Patrick a look he hoped the priest would interpret correctly. He did.

"Well," Patrick said, "Hugo and I can take a hint. Come on, Hugo. I'll tell you some more stories."

"Yay!" Hugo said.

As Patrick led Hugo away, Sangster said to Polly and Octavia, "Let's sit down."

They sat in the second pew while he sat in the first, turned to lean on the back and face them.

"Angela Grimes," he said. "Do you know who she is?"

"I think so," Polly said, but she deferred to her daughter. "'Tavia?"

"She's one of Isola's stuck up Garden District friends," Octavia said. Sangster noticed that the girl had slipped a sweater on over her skimpy top.

"Dat right," Polly said. She looked at Sangster. "Why?"

"She's dead."

"What?" Octavia said, loud enough to attract Father Patrick's attention from the back of the church momentarily.

"How?" Polly asked.

"Somebody strangled her, left her in the park in Jackson Square."

"Oh, no," Octavia said.

"What about Isola?" Polly asked. "Did you find her?"

"No."

"What about the other girls?" Octavia asked.

"No sign of them."

"The families must be so worried," Polly said. "Devastated."

Octavia snorted.

"What dat for, girl?"

"Those families don't care, Mama," Octavia said.

"Why you say dat?"

"Just ask Stark."

Polly looked at him.

"She's right," he said. "They're too busy. Haven't even reported them missing."

"Should I do dat, den?" Polly asked. "Report Isola missin'?"

"No need," Sangster said. "The police already talked to me."

"You gon' be workin' together?" Polly asked.

"Not exactly, but we'll all be looking for her."

"What about whoever killed Angela?" Octavia asked.

"That's the police's job," Sangster said. "I'm not a detective."

"You're looking for Isola, though," Octavia pointed out.

"I started out looking for whoever hurt Burke," he said. "I'm looking for your sister to help your mother, and because maybe she knows something."

"You t'ink whoever killed Angela hurt Burke?" Polly asked.

"Maybe," Sangster said. "That's what I'm going to find out." He looked at Octavia. "Now how about some of that gumbo?"

TWENTY-FIVE

Gumbo was not Sangster's favorite dish, but he did his best to do it justice for Mrs. Cox and for Octavia. He much preferred the etouffe the girl had made a couple of nights before, or jambalaya.

"That was great, Mrs. Cox."

"Thank Octavia," Mrs. Cox said. "She showed me how."

"I just pointed out a couple of things that would improve your own recipe, Mrs. Cox," Octavia said. Sangster was surprised at how gracious she was being.

Mrs. Cox smiled at Octavia, then returned to the kitchen. Patrick and Hugo were still in the church, and the doors were locked. Sangster sat at the table with Polly and Octavia, who drank tea while he ate.

"Polly, did you see Burke today?" he asked.

"I did," she said. "He da same, my poor Burke."

"Okay," Sangster said, "listen to me. I need you to stay here at the church with your children for a few days. No visits to the hospital, and no going to work."

"I can't do dat. I gotta work."

"You have to stay inside, Polly, where it's safe."

Polly looked at Octavia, then back at Sangster.

"You t'ink whoever kill dat girl gon' come after me and mine?"

"I don't know," he said. "But I need to make sure you're safe." He didn't want to tell her about Quinlan. That was personal.

"Mama . . ." Octavia said.

"A-all right," Polly said. "I guess I can do dat for a couple of days."

"Good," Sangster said. "Now tell me, Polly, why is Isola interested in Voodoo?"

"I don't know," the woman said. "She jus' got real curious a couple of years ago, start askin' questions."

"Did you answer them?"

"I did," she said, "but soon I couldn't, and she started lookin' other places for answers."

"Why would she get involved with the girls from the Garden District?"

"She met them in the Quarter," Octavia said. "At one of the Voodoo shops. She told me they was interested in learning Voodoo, too."

"Voodoo?" he asked. "Or how to actually cast spells?"

"Both, I guess."

"Did you check dose shops?" Polly asked.

"I did," he said. "One of them told me they thought she was there, and bought some things."

"Things? What things?" Polly asked.

"He didn't remember, but he said she might have bought some spell bags?"

"I found de jimson weed in her room, but no spell bags," Polly said. "Dis not good, Stark. She shouldn't be messin wit' dat stuff."

"But it's not real, right?" he asked.

"Whether it real or not," Polly said, "some of dem t'ings is dangerous."

"What, you mean, like . . . poison?"

"Sure, some of dem poison," she said.

"Did you tell the doctor you think Burke was poisoned?" Sangster asked.

She frowned. "Not in dose words."

"I mentioned Voodoo," Sangster said, "but not poison. Maybe that would help get them on the right track."

"We can go to de hospital tomorrow—"

"No," he said, "not you, and why wait? I can try to get the doctor on the phone tonight." He looked at his watch. It was after nine p.m. "I better do that now."

At that point a door opened and closed and Patrick appeared, with Hugo in tow.

"What's going on?" he asked.

"I was just leaving," Sangster said.

"Really? I thought we'd play some chess."

"Sorry," Sangster said. "I've got to make a call before it gets much later."

"Can I come with you?" Octavia asked.

"No," Sangster and Polly said at the same time.

"Okayyyyy," Octavia said. "Geez."

"I'll be back tomorrow," Sangster said, heading for the door.

"Call and let us know what happens with the doctor!" Polly called after him.

"I will."

He waited until he got home, rather than use his disposable cell. He called the hospital and asked for Doctor Judd, was told that the doctor was not on duty.

"I can give you his service number," she said.

He thought a moment, then said, "Okay, let me have it, but can you also put me through to the emergency room?"

"Of course." She gave him the number, then switched him over.

"Emergency."

"Is Nurse Claire O'Malley on duty?"

"Yes, she is." The voice was female, and impersonal.

"Can she come to the phone?"

"Hold on."

He waited seven minutes, and then Nurse O'Malley came on the line.

"Hello? I'm really busy, so this better be important."

"Nurse O'Malley, this is Stark. I'm the friend of—"

Suddenly, her voice was anything but impersonal.

"I know who you are," she said. "What can I do for you?"

"I was trying to get ahold of Dr. Judd to give him some information, but he's not there."

"We can give you his service—"

"Yes, the other woman told me that," he said, "but I was wondering if I could tell you what I wanted to tell him, and then you could make sure he got it."

Silence.

"Nurse?"

"I have some conditions."

"What are they?"

"First, that you call me Claire."

"All right, Claire."

"And second, that you meet me at Café Du Monde for beignets."

"When?"

"One hour."

"I thought you said you were busy."

"I am," she said, "trying to get out of here in one hour. I haven't eaten in hours."

He could easily make Café Du Monde in an hour.

"I'll see you there."

TWENTY-SIX

Café Du Monde had more than one location scattered throughout the state in Mandeville, Covington, Kenner, and Metarie to name a few. There was even one on the Riverwalk Marketplace. But whenever someone in New Orleans said, "Meet me at Café Dumonde," they were talking about the original French Market location on Decatur St. One of the definite benefits of going to the original was that it was open twenty-four hours.

Sangster arrived at 9:50, found Nurse O'Malley waiting for him at a table with a cup of coffee, but no beignets. Not yet.

"I thought you were hungry," he said, joining her.

"Eating without you would have been rude."

A fortyish waitress came over and said to her with a smile, "You were right." She looked at Sangster. "What can I get you?"

"Coffee," he said, "black, no sugar."

"Beignets?"

"Two orders, please," Claire said.

"Comin' up."

As the waitress went off to fill their orders Claire told him, "You're supposed to drink the coffee with hot milk here."

"I could never get into that habit," he said. "What did she mean when she said, 'you were right?'"

"I told her my boyfriend was handsome in a dangerous looking way."

"Boyfriend?"

She smiled. It made her pretty.

"Allow a girl her fantasies," she said. "First I made a fool of myself the other day thinking you came back to the hospital to see me, and tonight you called me because you couldn't get ahold of Dr. Judd. You don't do a lot for a girl's confidence."

"I'm sorry," Sangster said, for want of anything clever.

"Well," she said, "you're here. That's something."

She hadn't dressed for a date that morning as she prepared for work. As a result she wore a T-shirt with capped sleeves, jeans, sandals, carrying a straw purse that looked big enough to hold a picnic. She had taken the time, though, to fix her hair in the hospital locker room. It was naturally wavy, and she had put it into a ponytail.

Last year Sangster had become involved with a woman who owned a club in the Quarter, and she ended up dead. He hadn't been with a woman since.

"Yes," he said, "I'm here, and I'm really not very good at this."

"Well then," she said, "why don't we start over?" She stuck her hand out. "Hi, I'm Claire."

He took her hand, shook it, and lied. How could you build a relationship on that?

He wanted to say, "My name is Sangster. I used to kill people, but now I have a soul."

Instead he told her, "Stark, Richard Stark. Just don't call me Dick."

They talked over their beignets, and then asked for another order that they split, and more coffee.

She told him about her childhood in Bossier City, her education, training, and work as an ER nurse.

"Stark," she said, because he'd told her to call him

that, "I've been talking this whole time, and you haven't said a word about yourself."

"Well, that's because there's not much to tell," Sangster said. "I'm . . . retired."

"Really?" she asked. "You're too young to retire. What'd you retire from."

He hesitated, then said, "Public service."

"Ah, that explains it," she said. "Those Federal jobs, you can retire after twenty years, right? Or was it a city job?"

The waitress interrupted them at that point.

"Anything else?" she asked. "You two been talking for the better part of an hour."

"An hour?" Claire said. "Oh, shit, I've got to get back."

"Yeah," Sangster said. "I have to get going, too."

She started to dig into her bag and he said, "No, no, I've got it."

"Okay," she said, "I'm gonna let you."

He tossed some money down and she stood up, holding her bag over her shoulder.

"Hey, didn't you say there was something you were gonna tell me?" she asked.

"Yes, there was." He took her arm and they started walking. "I wanted to tell Dr. Judd to check my friend, Burke, for poison."

"You think somebody poisoned him?"

"It's possible."

"But . . . why?"

"I don't know," he said, when they reached her car. "That's what I'm trying to find out."

She used her key to open the driver's side door, then looked at him.

"That civil service job you mentioned," she said. "It wouldn't have been as a cop, would it?"

"What? A cop? No," he said, "no, I was never a policeman."

"Okay, mystery man." She leaned in and kissed him on the cheek. "I suppose I'll see you at the hospital, when you come to see your friend."

"Or," he said, "when I come to see you."

"There," she said, poking him in the chest with her forefinger. "You managed to say the right thing."

"Well," he said, "even a broken watch is right twice a day."

She laughed, got into her car, and drove away.

TWENTY-SEVEN

He drove directly to his house in Algiers, parked the car in front of Burke's. As he got to his door he stopped before sticking his key into the lock.

Something felt wrong.

He hadn't spotted Quinlan on his tail the whole day. And he was satisfied not to find anyone waiting for him on the porch. But something felt wrong. He studied the furniture on the porch. It appeared just as he'd left it after talking with Telemaco.

But this was Sangster's house. His instincts may not be what they once were, but he knew every inch of this house, how it looked and how it felt.

He backed away from the door, and down off the porch. He started to walk in a circle around the house. Maybe the whole Voodoo thing was starting to spook him. After all, Burke was in a coma that medical science couldn't understand. Yet again, with Polly mentioning poison, maybe she'd supplied the key to finding out what was ailing Burke, after all.

Sangster got around to the rear of the house, where there was a smaller porch leading to the back door. He didn't need a large back yard, so its small size had not been of concern to him when he rented the place.

He made his way to the back door, stopped and listened. He already knew that Quinlan had been in his house at least once. Was he inside again, waiting to make his move?

Sangster backed off the rear porch and made his way over to Burke's house. He let himself in, locking the door behind him. It was dark, but he didn't turn on a light. He just stood there and waited for his eyes to adjust, then went to a side window and peered out at his house. Maybe if he waited long enough, whoever was inside would reveal themselves. On the other hand, maybe nobody was inside and he was being paranoid because of what Quinlan had told him.

He settled into a chair and continued to watch. While he did so he thought about the incidents Quinlan had mentioned that had happened last year, in Vegas. Soul or no soul, Sangster had had very little choice in Vegas. It had been kill or be killed. He had tried to check with some holy men on how that jibed with having a soul, but so far he hadn't been able to reconcile it. He was determined not to kill again, but what was he to do if Quinlan came after him? And what about after Quinlan? Maybe his mistake had been coming back to Algiers, where he could be found.

He thought about Father Patrick. The priest was not like any of the other holy men—the Obeah Man in Vegas, some of the Baptist Ministers he'd talked with. Patrick was the first Catholic priest he'd spoken to since his soul made its sudden appearance. Maybe he was the man to talk the whole thing over with honestly. So far Burke was the only person who knew Sangster's story, and the somewhat religious ex-lawman had been very understanding. Could he expect less from a priest?

It was going on an hour and there had been no movement at his house. And then there it was. Someone had moved past a window, very briefly. If he hadn't been looking for it, he would have missed it. Was it a mistake? Or an invitation?

He moved away from the window, headed for the door, and stopped. Okay, so he didn't want to kill anyone, but going over there without a weapon was just plain foolish. He went to Burke's desk. He knew that in another part of the house Burke had a small armory, a collection of handguns he was very proud of. But instead of going there he opened the bottom desk drawer, took out something wrapped in cheesecloth. When he unwrapped it he was looking at a .45 caliber old west Peacemaker. Burke took good care of it, and Sangster knew that it worked just fine. He rummaged around in the bottom drawer, came up with six bullets. He loaded the weapon after first checking the action and dry-firing it to make sure it still worked. Once it was loaded he stuck it in his belt. He felt at once foolish, and like Wild Bill Hickok.

He left the house by the back, crossed over to his own back door, and went in . . .

Inside the house two men waited, one patiently, one not so patiently. If there was anything Claude and Basilio had learned from their Houngan it was patience. However, Basilio also suffered from a weak bladder, and it was he who passed in front of the window on the way to the bathroom.

"Again?" Claude asked.

"Hey," Basilio said, testily, "when I got to go I got go, *comprendre.*"

"Well, don't flush," Claude said. "I ain' gon' get killed because you can't hold your water, you."

"*Ki te'm anrepo'm,*" was Basilio's Creole response.

"I leave you alone when you stop dranin' your *zozo santi,*" Claude said, responding in kind.

"I got smelly dick?" Basilio said. "Your wife got *coco sal.*"

"My wife got smelly pussy?" Claude asked. "Your girlfriend got *coco vyeyi.*" To Claude's mind, an old pussy was worse than a smelly one. After all, weren't they all smelly? "Now *femin duol ou*," he said, telling his partner to shut up.

Basilio sulked, and realized he had to pee again.

Just as Sangster reached his back door and opened it a crack, he heard something. He stepped back and realized that he had heard the same sound earlier, when he stood at the front door. He'd unconsciously heard a sound, and hadn't identified it right away.

But he knew what it was now.

It was a toilet flushing.

TWENTY-EIGHT

Sangster slipped into the kitchen. He left Burke's gun in his belt. As he sniffed the air he could smell them. Incense. He'd never had incense in his house. It must have been on their clothing. To him that meant it wasn't Quinlan. He remembered the smell of it in Papa Legba's Gallery.

He moved to the kitchen door and peered around, into the living room. As he did, a figure entered the room, apparently adjusting his trousers.

"*Merde*, you flushed!" another man complained.

"What does it matter?" the first man asked. "No one is here but us."

As Sangster watched the second man took up his position, once again crossing in front of the window. They were concentrating on the front door. He was convinced that these men had been sent by someone connected to either Papa Legba's, or one of the other places he'd visited. They were definitely not pros.

He stepped into the room.

"You jokers want to tell me what you're doing in my house?"

Both men leaped to their feet. The larger one said, "Merde!" again, and the other, slimmer one farted audibly.

Both stood there, stunned. From what Sangster could see they did not seem to be carrying guns, so he let Burke's peacemaker remain in his belt, where the two men could see it.

"Tell me who sent you," Sangster said, "and then you can walk out."

The man who had come from the bathroom—the one who'd farted—looked anxiously at the other. It was clear who was in charge.

"You," Sangster said, pointing to the larger one. He was a big man, though not as big as Lloyd, from the gallery. "Who sent you?"

"*Pic kee toi*," the man spat. It didn't take much to figure out he'd just been told to go fuck himself.

"That's the wrong answer," Sangster said.

The big man tried another tactic.

"Do you think we were sent here to do you harm?" he asked in what Sangster now knew was a Creole accent.

"That's exactly what I think."

"No, my friend," he said, his voice deep, "we only came to talk to you."

"About what?"

"You want to know where the girl is, no?"

"Which girl?"

The man smiled and said very slowly, "I-so-la."

"You know where she is?"

"Maybe."

"And who killed the other girl?" Sangster said. "Angela Grimes."

"We do not know her."

"Is that a fact? You know Isola, but not Angela?"

"I-so-la is Creole." As if that explained it all.

"What are the two of you doing here?"

"Like I said. We came to talk."

"What's your names?"

"I am Claude," the bigger man said. "This is Basilio."

"You know a man named Lloyd? A woman named Kate?"

Claude frowned. "No."

"Okay then," Sangster said, "you wanted to talk to me, so talk."

His eyes had adjusted, but it was still dark in the room. Sangster liked to contribute what happened next to that, and not to the erosion of his skills.

He surmised later that the thinner man had been watching the other man closely, and when one moved, so did the other.

The big man charged, surprising him. Sangster went for the gun in his belt, but before he could draw it the man crashed into him.

The second man ran for the window and launched himself through it. Broken glass followed him out. That couldn't have been what the big man expected.

The impact drove Sangster back into the kitchen. He and Claude rolled around together on the floor. The breath had been driven from his body, but he couldn't afford to let that stop him from struggling.

Claude was stronger than he was, but Sangster had superior flexibility. The big man tried to crush Sangster beneath his weight, but the ex-hitman slid out from beneath him and, still on his back, kicked out at the man. His heel caught Claude on the side of the head, stunning him. Sangster had time to pull the gun from his waistband. There was a time he wouldn't have hesitated to use it to end the fight, but he pointed it at the ceiling and pulled the trigger.

The big man moved quickly, despite the dizziness he must have felt from the kick. He got to the back door, slammed it open and ran out.

Sangster struggled to his feet and ran after him, still trying to catch his breath. He heard the man running alongside the house toward the front and followed. He didn't know where the second man was, but given the way he dove out the window, he was probably most of the way to the ferry by now.

He ran, crunching broken glass beneath his feet, the gun still in his hand. It had been dark in the house, but was dusk outside. He could hear the man running, but couldn't see him. Sangster ran past the front porch, eyeballed the street, didn't see anyone. When he heard the sound behind him he started to turn, but knew it was too late. At least that instinct hadn't left him. He tensed for the impact, and heard the shot.

TWENTY-NINE

"So you don't know where the shot came from?"

The police who responded to his call were from both the Jefferson Parish Sheriff's Department in Harvey, and the New Orleans P.D.'s 4th District's new digs on Sanctuary Drive. He was facing several cops with notebooks, but the one speaking was from the NOPD.

Sets of portable lights had been set up to illuminate the scene. Cops and techs in white suits, boots and gloves were studying the area. They were also inside the house, probably turning it inside out.

"No," Sangster said. "I heard the shot, but I couldn't tell where it came from."

"All right," the uniformed cop said, "let me get this straight, then. You came home, found two men in your house, tussled with them—"

"One of them," Sangster interrupted. "The other one ran."

"Okay, so you wrestled with one, he lit out the back door and you took off after him."

"Right."

"Then this one came up from behind you and somebody saved your bacon, shooting him before he could stick a knife in your back."

"I guess."

They all looked down at the dead man, the slender one who had jumped out the window. Sangster figured he was hiding underneath the porch, and when Sangster ran by, he slithered out with his knife.

"Say," one of the Sheriff's men said, "ain't that Burke's house next door? The former Sheriff?"

"That's right," Sangster said.

"Could it be him who shot this fella?"

"No," Sangster said, "he's in the hospital."

"Okay," the NOPD cop said, "we'll get this guy removed for you. You might as well hang out on the porch."

"Sure," Sangster said.

He had gone inside to call 911—like any good citizen would—and had taken the time to stow Burke's gun away. He hoped a cop wouldn't open the wrong drawer and find it.

He went up onto the porch and sat where he usually sat to play chess with Burke. The front door opened and a man came out carrying two bottles of Blackened Voodoo.

"Here you go," he said.

"Where'd you come from?" Sangster asked, accepting the beer.

Detective Telemaco sat in Burke's chair.

"This isn't your district," Sangster said.

"No," Telemaco said, "I'm in the Eighth, but I put out the word that I should hear about anything going on around Burke's house."

"And mine?"

Telemaco shrugged.

"I didn't even see you get here," Sangster said.

"Ya'll were busy being questioned," Telemaco said, gesturing with the bottle. "You mind talking to me?"

"Why not?" Sangster said. "You brought me a beer, didn't you? Ask away."

"You know this guy?"

"No."

"The guy who was with him?"

"Nope."

"Ever see either of them before?"

"Never."

"Do you think this has anything to do with what happened to Burke?"

"I don't know, and they weren't talking. Just . . . attacking."

"Maybe it has something to do with what happened in Vegas last year."

Sangster thought about Quinlan and said, "No, I don't know."

"What *do* you know, Stark?"

"Just what I told the other cops," Sangster said, with a shrug. "I came home, found these two guys in my house and they attacked me."

"Seems like you did pretty well in a two against one situation."

"Well," Sangster said, "one of them ran—or, I thought he ran. Turns out he was hiding. When I ran by, chasing the other one, he came up behind me with a knife. I figure he was under the porch."

"And somebody bailed you out. Any idea who?"

"No."

"Any idea where the shot came from?"

"No," Sangster said.

"According to the tech guys it looks like it came from the direction of Burke's house."

"If you say so."

"Of course," Telemaco said, "one of the Jefferson Parish guys thinks that you might have hid from him and shot him from that direction."

"I'd need a gun for that," Sangster said. "Did they find one?"

"No," Telemaco said, "I told them I didn't think it went that way, but they're still looking."

"Thanks for the vote of confidence."

Telemaco took a drink from his bottle and said,

"Why don't we just sit here, drink our beers, and see what they come up with—if anything."

Sangster raised his bottle and said, "Sounds like a good idea to me."

THIRTY

They had a second beer while they waited for the techs to finish and dismantle the lighting, the detectives and medical examiner to complete their jobs, and the body to be removed. In the end, an NOPD Patrol Captain came by to sign off on the scene, and all the law enforcement personnel cleared out, leaving Telemaco and Sangster on the porch. Sangster had agreed to appear at the Jefferson Parish location to sign a statement, which would be forwarded to the NOPD.

"It's so quiet," Telemaco said. "Is it always this quiet?"

"And why are you still here?" Sangster asked, instead of answering.

"Just finishing my beer."

"Are you even on duty?"

"I'm always on duty."

"So, am I off the hook for this shooting?"

"The Fourth District detective will do an investigation, but I don't see why not. You'll just have to wait for it to be official."

Sangster rubbed one hand over his face.

"Are you okay?" the detective asked. "Did anybody offer you medical attention?"

"Yeah, they did," Sangster said, "but I'm fine. I just rolled around on the floor with one of them, and then he ran, too."

Telemaco put his empty bottle down on the chess table and stood up.

"Do ya'll have anything else to tell me about those two?" he asked. "Anything ya'll might have noticed?"

He could have told the man they were Creole, or that they smelled of incense, or that they insinuated they knew where Isola Bourque was, but he decided not to tell him any of it.

"No, nothing," he said. "It all happened too fast."

"Well, I'll have to take your word for it, for now," the detective said. "If ya'll decide there's something ya'll want to tell me, let me know."

"How are you doing with your investigation? About Burke, I mean."

"We're trying to retrace Burke's steps through the Quarter," Telemaco said, "trying to find out what took him to Pirates Alley."

"The Cathedral?" Sangster suggested.

"It was locked."

"Did you talk to the people there?" Sangster said. "The priests, or whoever—"

"Yeah, we did," Telemaco said. "They don't know any Ken Burke. Nobody else saw anything, because the café and the bookstore were closed."

"Do you have an update on his condition?" Sangster asked.

"The same, last I heard," the detective said.

Telemaco took a few steps off the porch, then turned.

"Ya'll got a spare key to Burke's house?"

"I do."

"Can we have a look?"

"You know," Sangster said, "nobody else asked that."

* * *

They entered the house and turned on the lights. Sangster stayed by the switch while Telemaco walked around.

"Somebody was in here," Telemaco said.

Yes, Sangster thought, *me,* but he didn't say anything.

"How can you tell?" he asked, instead.

"See the curtain?" the detective said. Sangster saw that he'd left the curtain partially drawn back. "Somebody was watching your house."

Again Sangster thought, *me.* Careless of him to have left the curtain like that.

"And it looks like somebody went through this desk." Telemaco opened the drawers, peered in and closed them. When he came to the one the gun had been in he reached inside and took out a bullet. "Do you know what was in this drawer?"

"No."

"Could it have been a gun?"

"Maybe," Sangster said. "Burke collected them."

"Do you know where they are?"

"He keeps them in a case in the other room."

"Can ya'll show me?" He closed the drawer, but kept the bullet.

"Sure, this way."

Sangster led Telemaco to a door and opened it. There were several gun cases, one of which was mounted on the wall and filled with rifles. The others were set against the wall and filled with pistols and automatics from all time periods.

"Doesn't look like any are missing," Telemaco said. "All the cases are locked, and the glass is intact." He peered into the handgun cases. "He's got some nice pieces here."

Sangster knew that the Peacemaker was Burke's

favorite. He never kept it in the gun case, and always made sure it was in good working order.

"You thought someone broke in here and used one of Burke's guns to save me?"

"It was just a thought."

"Kind of a wild one, don't you think?" Sangster asked. "Who would do that?"

"I don't know," Telemaco said. "Maybe an old friend? From an old life?"

"An old life?"

Telemaco held up his hands. "Look, with everything that happened last year I just thought—but okay, let's not go there right now. Maybe this isn't the time."

"Yeah," Sangster said, "okay."

They turned off the light, left the room and closed the door. Then they did the same with the other lights and the front door.

They walked back to Sangster's house, where Telemaco turned to look back at Burke's.

"I suppose that shot could have been made from that window."

"Or the porch," Sangster said, and when the detective looked at him he added, "right?"

"Possibly."

Telemaco seemed to be giving the matter more thought.

"Detective, tell me something."

"What?"

"Why wasn't I taken in tonight?" Sangster asked. "For questioning, and to sign a statement? Wouldn't that have been normal?"

"Well," Telemaco said, "maybe I spoke up for you, vouched for you. You are going in tomorrow to make a statement though, right?"

"That's right."

"There ya'll go, then," the detective said. "No harm done."

"I appreciate it," Sangster said. "What's happening with the other case? The dead girl?"

"I'm not working it," Telemaco said, "but I'm keeping track of any progress. Nothing yet."

"What about the other girls?" Sangster asked. "Have the parents heard anything?"

"No, nothing."

"I'll bet they're not even concerned," Sangster said. "Too much on their minds."

"You're probably right. Okay, Stark, I guess I'll see you when I see you. You have my number."

"Yes, I do."

"Do yourself a favor," Telemaco said, "don't hesitate to use it."

Sangster sat where he was until he figured Telemaco was on the ferry, then picked up the two empty beer bottles and took them into the house.

THIRTY-ONE

Sangster had to do some cleaning up. He didn't know who had made a bigger mess, the intruders, or the cops and techs. He took the empty bottles into the kitchen—which was even more of a mess—and threw them in the trash. As he did so he spotted something behind the trash can. He picked it up, saw that it was some kind of bag. In fact, it looked like something he'd seen at the Voodoo museum. Had it fallen out of the big man's pocket while they were struggling on the floor?

It was more a pouch than a bag, made of leather, etched with words in what appeared to be verses. He didn't open it.

He found a small paper bag, and put the item in it, then left the house by the back door, taking it with him.

As he drove to the church he thought about Quinlan. The hitman was the only person he could think of who might have taken that shot. But why would Quinlan bail him out that way? Just to save Sangster for himself? He'd have to find the man and ask him.

He stopped his car in front of the church and walked up to the rectory door. Mrs. Cox answered it and greeted him very warmly.

"Have you come back for more of my cooking?" she asked. "That clever young girl has shown me some other things."

"I could use a bite," he admitted, "but I really came to check on Polly and the kids."

"Come in, then," she said. "They're in the sitting room. Except for the boy. He's asleep."

"And Father Patrick?"

"He's hearing late confessions in the church," she told him.

He followed her into the comfortable room, where Polly and Octavia were sitting. The mother was reading a book, while the daughter was staring off into space. But when she saw Sangster her eyes lit up.

"Finally!" she said, jumping up out of her chair and rushing to him. "I'm so bored! There's no TV here."

"Nice to see you, too, Octavia," he said.

"Stark," Polly said, lowering her book. "Girl, give de man some space."

Octavia reluctantly backed away a few steps. He noticed she was wearing a plain short-sleeved T-shirt, and had a bra on underneath. Maybe Father Patrick had a talk with her about the way she dressed?

"Can you take me out of here for a while?" she asked him. "I need some air."

"You're safer here," he told her.

"Oooh," she moaned. "Everybody's tellin' me that."

"'Tavia," Polly said, "why don't you help Mrs. Cox fix something for Stark to eat as a midnight snack?"

Octavia rolled her eyes and said, "Yes, Mama."

She and Mrs. Cox left the room.

Sangster approached Polly, who laid her book aside. Sangster couldn't see the title. He wondered if it was one he had already read. He spent a lot of his time now reading. Of the few times he still went to the Quarter it was to go to a bookstore.

"What is in de bag?" she asked.

"Maybe you could tell me."

He handed it to her. She opened the bag with a frown, peered inside, then carefully took out the pouch.

"Is it what I think it is?" he asked.

"A gris-gris bag." She set it aside. "Where you get it?"

"Two Creole men were waiting for me in my house tonight," he said. "I fought with them. One of them dropped this."

"You fought dem?" she asked. "Dey got away?"

"One did," he said. "One's dead."

"You killed him?"

He shook his head.

"Someone else shot him. Saved my life."

"Who shot him?"

"I don't know," he said. "I have an idea, but I don't know for sure."

"Why you bring dat to me?"

"Just to make sure I was right."

"And now dat you are?"

"I have an idea where to go next."

She looked at the bag.

"You did not open it."

"Neither did you."

She sniffed.

"Not my place."

"Is it mine?"

"More den mine."

"What will I find?"

"Some t'ings," she said. "Maybe personal t'ings. A certain number of dem. Was dere a doll?"

"No," he said, "no doll. Should there have been?"

"Sometimes dere's a doll."

"So they were going to try to . . . what? Put some kind of spell on me?"

"Maybe." She hesitated before continuing. "You need ask somebody who know more den I do."

Sangster walked to the pouch, picked it up and put it back in the paper bag. Then he set it aside to deal with later.

"I'll do that."

"Come," she said, getting up. "You need eat."

He didn't argue. Whatever they had cooked smelled good.

THIRTY-TWO

It was jambalaya.

While he was eating, Father Patrick came in from hearing confessions and sat down with him to have a bite.

"Hear any interesting confessions, Father?" Octavia asked him.

"I can't tell you that, Octavia," he said. "I'm bound by the seal of the confessional."

"I didn't ask you what they told you," she pointed out with a shrug. "I just asked if it was interesting."

"Oh," Patrick said, "well, in that case . . . they're usually very boring. One or two might be interesting, I guess"

"I'm gonna go take a bath," she announced, and left the kitchen.

"I gon' read my book," Polly said, and followed Octavia out.

"I'm gonna . . ." Mrs. Cox said, but she just stopped, shook her head, and left the room.

"More wine?" Patrick asked.

"Sure."

The priest poured more red wine into their glasses.

"It's not . . ." Sangster said.

". . . sacramental wine? No. We keep that in the church sacristy."

Sangster took a drink, then went back to the jambalaya, which was every bit as good as the food had been the night before.

Sangster finished telling Patrick what had happened at his house, then asked, "Tell me about confession."

"What do you want to know?"

"Do you have to have a soul to confess?"

"Catholics believe everyone has a soul, Stark."

"But you have to be Catholic to confess."

"Yes."

"And are Catholics forgiven for any sin? No matter how bad?"

"As long as you're sincere in your confession, and truly have remorse for sinning against God, then yes, they are forgiven."

"For anything?" Sangster asked again.

"Yes," Patrick said, "anything."

After they ate for a few more moments Sangster asked, "Do you know what a soul looks like?"

"No," Patrick said, "nobody knows that."

"Then how do you know you have one?"

"I told you," Patrick said, "all Catholics believe they have souls. They don't need to see them."

Sangster noticed that Father Patrick usually prefaced his answers with "all Catholics believe" not "I" believe.

"That takes a lot of . . ." He groped for a word.

"Faith," Patrick said, "is the word you're looking for."

"I suppose."

"Do you have faith in anything, Stark?"

"I used to."

"In what?"

Sangster took another sip of wine and said, "Myself."

After a few moments Patrick said, "Let's talk about your soul."

"What about it?"

"How does it make you different?"

Sangster stared at the priest, looking for the right

words. He remembered waking that morning, filled with shame for the things he had done. He'd once been described by an employer as a "soulless" killer who never felt a hint of remorse. Since he was feeling it that morning, he'd assumed that he suddenly had a soul.

But maybe he was wrong.

"I don't know, Patrick," he said. "It's hard to describe." At least, it was hard without actually telling Father Patrick what he used to do.

"I'm going to assume that what you used to do," Patrick said, as if reading Sangster's mind, "was against the law."

Sangster didn't respond to that directly. Instead he said, "I woke up one morning and could no longer lead the life I'd been leading."

"And you attribute that to the sudden appearance of a soul?"

"What else?"

"A conscience?"

"Can I have one without the other?"

Now it was Father Patrick who didn't respond right away.

"You know," he said, "that's a damned good question."

Sangster put his fork down and stared across the table at his new friend.

"Let me ask you something."

"Go ahead."

"If I converted to the Catholic religion," he asked, "could I then confess to the things I've done and be forgiven?"

Patrick hesitated, then said, "First, you'd have to believe in religion. Next, you'd have to feel honest remorse for the things you did, and not just be confessing to get out from under the guilt. Could you do that?"

"I don't know."

"I've noticed something about you, Stark."

"What?"

"You don't react to much. I mean, you don't show much emotion. Is that something that comes naturally to you?"

"I guess so," Sangster said, with a shrug. "I've never seen the sense in overreacting to things."

"But . . ., you've got to react to something. How do you feel about your friend Burke being hurt?"

Sangster thought about it a moment, then said, "Angry."

"And what did that anger make you do?"

"What do you mean?"

"Throw something? Punch a wall? Yell?"

"None of those things."

"Then what?"

Sangster shrugged. "I'm just trying to find the people who did it to him."

"Well," Patrick said, "I'm sure I wouldn't want to be them when you do."

After they finished eating they left Mrs. Cox to clean up and went to join Polly in the sitting room. Octavia was nowhere to be seen.

"Where's 'Tavia?" Sangster asked.

"Still upstairs," Polly said.

"She wouldn't leave the building, would she?" he asked.

"I t'ink she scared enough to stay," Polly said, "even if she is bored."

"Is that it?" Patrick asked, pointing to the paper bag. "The gris-gris pouch?"

"Yes," Sangster said.

"Can I . . ."

"Sure."

Patrick walked over and took the pouch out of the paper bag. He turned it over in his hands, examining it.

"It's beautiful work."

"Yes, it is," Sangster agreed.

"What's in it?"

"I don't know," Sangster said.

Father Patrick looked at Polly.

"How would I know?"

"Can we look inside?"

"Not our place," Polly said. "Dat up to Stark."

Now Patrick looked at Stark.

"What do you think?" he asked. "Want to look inside?"

"No."

"Really?" the priest asked. "You're not even curious?"

"Not even a little."

"Well," Patrick said, with a shrug, "I guess it's up to you." He put it back in the bag.

"I better get going," Sangster said. "Polly, did you see Burke today?"

"Yes," she said. "Dere's no change. He just lies dere."

"I'll go and see him tomorrow. Do you want a lift?"

"I got work to do in the mornin'," she said. "I'll go in de afternoon."

"Okay," he said. "Then I'll say goodnight."

"Don't forget this," Patrick said, picking up the bag and handing it to him.

"Thanks."

"Father?" Mrs. Cox called.

"Coming, Mrs. Cox. See you tomorrow, Stark?"

"Sure. 'night, Polly."

"Good-night, Stark."

Sangster walked to the front door on his own. He found Octavia waiting there for him.

"You goin' back to the Papa Legba tomorrow?" she asked.

"What makes you ask that?"

"You wanna find out about the gris-gris, right?"

"Just who sent it," he said, "not what's in it."

"Can I go?"

"No."

"I can translate if you run into Creole."

He started to say no again, then stopped.

"And I know those other girls on sight," she added.

"All right," he said. "Meet me out front at eight a.m."

She squealed and gave him a quick hug.

Back at his house he sat in the dark on the porch with a bottle of beer. He didn't think anyone would make another try for him that night.

Apparently, somebody didn't want him finding Isola Bourque—and, in fact, did not even want him looking for her. He didn't know if the two Creole's were there to deliver a warning, or some kind of Voodoo spell. He stared at the gris-gris bag on the table in front of him and still had no desire to open it. He did, however, want to know who sent it. What kind of Voodoo Priest or Priestess had he pissed off just by looking for a missing little girl?

And then there was Quinlan. The hitman had pretty much issued an open challenge to him and then—if he was right—had been around to save his life tonight. According to what Mickey had told him, Quinlan was somebody to take very seriously. And Mickey was also right that he was out of practice. That was, however, by choice. And he wasn't in a hurry to get back into practice any time soon.

He was going to have to figure out a way to deal with Quinlan.

THIRTY-THREE

Sangster picked Octavia up in front of the rectory the next morning, then drove to the office of the Jefferson Parish Sheriff. He left the girl in the car while he went inside to make his statement.

"Is this everything you remember, Mr. Stark?" the detective asked him.

"It is."

"This is an official statement," the man said. "If there's anything here that's not honest—"

"Detective," Sangster said, "I assure you, that's as honest as I can be."

The man, middle-aged and cynical, said, "Yeah, okay, then sign it."

Sangster signed and got out of there.

"Everythin' okay?" Octavia asked when he came back to the car.

"As okay as it's going to get."

He drove to the ferry and, while they rode across to Canal Street, kept his eyes peeled for any sign of Quinlan.

"So where is it?" she asked, on the ferry. They were standing outside the car, leaning against it.

"Where's what?"

"The gris-gris."

"It's in my house."

"Did you even look inside?"

"No."

"Why not?"

"I told you last night," he said, "I'm not curious."

"Is that because you don't believe?"

"Probably."

"Why do you keep looking around?"

He glanced at her. "Because I'm careful."

"Did those two men come after you last night because you're looking for my sister?"

"Why else?"

She shrugged. "I don't know. Maybe because you're . . ."

"I'm what?"

She shrugged again. "I don't know."

"If you've got something to ask me, Octavia, then ask," he told her.

"Okay," she said. "You're not a cop. Are you some kind of a . . . criminal?"

"What makes you ask that?"

"Because nothing scares you."

"You think not?"

"I know it," she said.

"Well," he said, "I'm not a criminal." *Not anymore,* he thought.

"Do you know about . . . guns, and things?"

"A little."

"So were you ever a soldier?"

"I was," he said, "but not for very long."

"'Cause I feel safe with you. Safer than I do at the church with Father Patrick."

"Father Patrick's a good man."

"Sure he is," she said. "And he's not like any other priest I ever met. But he ain't you."

"How many other priests have you met?"

"A few," she said. "I've had some friends who were Catholic."

"I haven't known many priests," he admitted. "What makes him different?"

"Well, for one thing," she said, "the way he looks at me."

Sangster looked at her. She was back to wearing her skimpy top, without a bra.

"How's that?"

"The same way you look at me," she said. "It's not the way most men do."

"That's because of the way you dress, and you're young enough to be my daughter."

She smiled. "It's because I'm a pretty girl, no matter how I dress. Only you and Father Patrick look at me like I'm a kid."

"You are a kid."

"But don't you think I'm pretty?"

"Sure," he said, "you're a pretty kid."

"Do you have a girlfriend?"

"No."

"Why not?"

"Get back in the car," he said. "We're docking."

They drove directly into the Quarter.

"Are we going to Papa Legba's again?" Octavia asked.

"Yes."

"Do you think those men were sent from there?"

"There," he said, "or from Marie Laveau's. Or maybe the Museum, but I doubt that."

This time he parked down the street from the gallery, and not in front.

"Okay, you—"

"I know," she said. "Stay in the car."

"Smart," he said, "and pretty."

THIRTY-FOUR

Sangster walked down the street toward the Papa Legba Gallery. He was fairly sure Quinlan was nowhere around. Knowing that made him even more nervous about what the man was planning.

As he approached the gallery he decided that going in the front door—again—was not a good idea.

While many of the buildings in the French Quarter are of French and Spanish architecture, there are a few Colonial era buildings. The building which housed the Papa Legba was one of these, dating back to the 1790's. The gallery itself was on the first floor, a warehouse area on the second, and the third was a residence.

There was a *porte-cochere*—or carriageway—along one side, which worked perfectly for Sangster. He followed the carriageway to the rear of the building. What tourists to the French Quarter don't often see are the rear balconies and galleries, as well as the gardens behind the buildings. This particular structure had a beautiful garden and balconies on every level.

Sangster looked around carefully, making sure there was no one lurking in the garden, before making his way to the back door. It was locked, but that wasn't a problem. Picking locks was a talent he hadn't lost. He didn't carry a full set of lock picks, but he did carry the two pieces he needed: a hooked diamond pick and a tension tool. He didn't carry them all the time, but this had seemed like a day he might need them.

He put the tools to work and unlocked the back door in minutes. With the picks back in his wallet, he opened the door slowly, peered in and entered.

Once inside he paused and listened. He heard the drone of voices, but couldn't make out what they were saying. He wasn't even sure which floor they were coming from. All he could tell was that one sounded like a man and one a woman—Kate and Lloyd? Maybe.

He was in a hallway. Following it one way would take him toward the front of the building. The other way was a stairway going up. Since he knew what was on the first floor—the gallery, a back room, and this hallway—he decided to go up.

He moved to the stairway, tested the first two steps with his weight to see if they would make any sound. They seemed solid, so he started to ascend.

He counted ten steps then reached the top. Another hallway, which he followed to a room that seemed to run the entire length of the building.

The room was large enough to be a warehouse, but the majority of the space was empty. He walked about, gently in case the floor creaked. Against one wall were some pieces of art in storage cases that took up little room. One section of the floor bore some odd marks, almost like charring, as if someone had been building fires there.

He went back to the hall, found the stairs to the third floor, and ascended again. This time he came to another door right at the head of the steps.

Crouching down, he employed his lock picks again. When he had the door open he slipped inside. Unlike the second floor, this one was air-conditioned. With his picks once again stowed away, he looked around. It was an apartment—an expensively furnished one. There were floor to ceiling windows in the front and along the back wall, covered with French doors leading out to the balconies.

Sangster decided that whoever lived there must own

the gallery. That was the person he wanted to speak with, so he decided to wait. He just hoped Octavia would not get impatient in the car.

He went to the front window and looked down at the street. There were people walking by, but no sign of Quinlan. Was the man smart enough to keep out of sight even though Sangster was looking for him? He hoped not. He didn't need the hitman to be that good.

Octavia opened the window of the car, rather than starting the engine to run the air conditioner. She was startled when a man appeared at the open window.

"Hello," he said.

She started.

"Sorry," the man said, "I didn't mean to scare you."

"You didn't," she said. "Just surprised me, is all."

"Maybe you can help me."

"How?" She eyed him suspiciously. He was tall, dark and mean looking.

"I'm looking for the Napoleon House. Do you know where that is?"

"I do," she said. "St. Charles and St. Louis. On the corner."

"Thanks," he said. "What are you doin' here by yourself, pretty little girl like you?"

She leaned out the window, so he could get a good look at her little tits. And he looked, backing away from the car so he could get a better view.

"You think I'm pretty?" she asked.

"You know you are," he said, "you're a sexy, pretty little girl."

"I ain't no little girl."

"How old are you?"

She lifted her chin and said, "I'm eighteen."

He laughed at her. "You're maybe . . . fourteen, if you're a day."

"Hmph. I don't act fourteen."

"No," he said, "you don't."

She narrowed her eyes. "What do you really want? You ain't lookin' for the Napoleon House."

"Smart girl," he said. "You're right. I'm not looking for it—although I could use a drink."

"Me, too."

He laughed. "Not a chance. I have enough trouble in my life as it is."

"What *do* you want?" she asked.

"I'm lookin' for a friend of yours."

"Who's that?"

"His name," Quinlan said, "is Sangster—well, I guess you know him as Stark."

THIRTY-FIVE

While Sangster waited he had a look around. The place was very neat, almost unlived in. No dirty dishes, no laundry, no personal papers. And there was no Voodoo paraphernalia anywhere. He was starting to think his assumption was wrong. Perhaps the owner didn't actually live there. Maybe it was just a temporary apartment, one that was kept for guests.

He was about to give up after half-an-hour when he heard the front door lock. As the door opened he ducked out of sight behind it. The woman he'd spoken to twice so far, Kate, entered. She heaved a tired sigh, closed the door and was startled to see him standing there.

"How did you get in here?" Kate asked.

"Quietly," he said. "I thought we should have a talk."

"About what?"

"A dead man and a gris-gris bag."

"I don't know anything about a dead man," she said. "What do you want to know about gris-gris bags?"

"Not bags in general," he said. "A particular gris-gris bag." He'd worn a wind breaker that day, even though it was too warm for it. But he had need of the pockets. He took the gris-gris from the pocket and said, "This one."

She stared down at it. "It's beautiful work."

"Yes, it is."

"You mind if I get a drink?"

"No, I don't mind."

She walked to a table near the front windows. It was one of those that folded out into a small bar, complete with a decanter.

"Would you like something?"

"I don't know that I'd be comfortable drinking anything you gave me."

She laughed and turned to face him holding a glass.

"Afraid I'll give you some Voodoo potion?"

"Yes," he said. "Now what about this bag?"

"What about it?"

"Did it come from here?"

"I told you before," she said. "We're a gallery. We don't sell Voodoo crap."

"I wasn't thinking that you sold it," he said. "I was thinking that you sent a couple of men to deliver it."

"Why would I do that?"

"Maybe because you're a *mambo*?"

"Even if I was a Voodoo priestess," she said, calmly, "why would I send you a gris-gris?"

"That's what I'm here to find out."

"Well," she said, folding her arms with the glass in her right hand, "you won't find out from me."

"You speak . . . oddly"' he said. "I noticed it when I first met you."

"What do you mean, odd?"

"No accent."

"And what did you expect? Creole? Jamaican?"

"Something," he said. "You speak like you've been trained not to sound like . . . well, you're from nowhere."

"What else can I do for you, Mr. . . . . have you ever told me your name?"

"I don't think you ever asked. It's Stark."

"What else can I do for you, Mr. Stark?"

"Where's your man Lloyd?" he asked. "Maybe he knows a little something about the two men who came to my house with this bag."

"Two men?" she repeated. "I thought you said there was a dead man?"

"That's right," he said. "One of them ended up dead."

"And the other one?"

"He got away."

"That's too bad."

"That one of them was killed?" he asked. "Or that one of them got away?"

"Well . . . both, I suppose." She sipped her drink. "Did you kill him?"

"No."

"Who did?"

"I don't know."

She sipped her drink again. He waited, but she didn't continue.

"You're not very curious," he said.

"As I told you," she replied, "I don't know anything about the two men or the gris-gris bag. I only asked a couple of questions to be . . . polite."

"Polite to someone who broke into your building? Your apartment?"

"I can't very well physically throw you out," she said. "And Lloyd wouldn't hear me yell from here."

"Still, you're very calm about all this."

"I've worked in the French Quarter a very long time," she said.

"I guess we're not all what we seem," he said.

She sipped her drink and then asked, "Are you talking about me, or yourself?"

THIRTY-SIX

"Who's Sangster?"

Sangster didn't react, he kept driving with his eyes on the street.

"Where'd you hear that name?"

"From a man." Octavia said.

"What man?"

She shrugged. "I don't know. Just a man who came up to the car and talked to me."

"Did he say his name?"

"No."

"What did he want?"

"Well," she answered, "he asked for directions, but then we talked a while and he finally said he was looking for you. Only he called you Sangster, and said I probably knew you as Stark."

"What did he look like?"

"He was tall, a little younger than you, dark-hair, kinda rough lookin'. Maybe even a little sexy."

"What did you tell him, Octavia?"

"I said I didn't know what he was talkin' about."

"And?"

"He said I was a sexy little girl and he went away."

Sangster figured that approaching Octavia and engaging her in conversation was another message from Quinlan who—to this point—was happy playing mind games. First, approaching him outside the museum, then saving his life with one well-placed shot, and now this. Sangster had never played mind games with a target. He always had too much respect for them. Perhaps that could be Quinlan's undoing.

"Do you know him?" Octavia asked. "The sexy man?"

"I know him."

"Is he a friend of yours?" she asked. "Should I have told him where you were?"

"No," he said, "no, you shouldn't have. In fact, you shouldn't ever talk to him again."

"He said I was sexy."

He looked at her for the first time. She smiled at him.

"You already know that, Octavia."

"Yeah, I do."

He pulled the car to a stop down the street from Marie Laveau's.

"Stay in the car?" she asked.

"You got it."

"Why are you wearing that jacket?" she asked. "Aren't you hot?"

"Very," he said. "I need the pockets."

"You brought it with you, didn't you?"

"Yeah," he said. "So I could find out who sent it."

"Maybe we should look inside."

"Do you know what's inside a gris-gris bag?"

"No," she said, "but Isola would."

"Tell me something, Octavia," Sangster said. "If your sister could, do you think she'd call your mother?"

"You mean do I think she went off on her own, or was she kidnapped?"

"That's what I'm trying to figure out."

"This *is* the longest she's ever gone without contacting us." She suddenly grabbed his arm. "You don't think she's dead, like that other girl, do you?"

"Is this the first time you considered that?"

"Well . . . yes."

He patted her hand, which was still grasping his arm.

"Just wait here—and don't talk—"

"What?"

"On second thought . . ." If he left her out there, Quinlan could show up again. He obviously had no trouble finding them the first time. Maybe he had put a locater on the car.

"Stark?"

"Come with me," he said. "Come on."

"All right!" She happily got out of the car.

As they walked up the street to Marie Laveau's, Octavia asked, "Do you think the other girls are dead, too?"

"I hope not," he said.

When they reached the storefront he thought about trying to break in the back way again, then decided against it. Maybe the direct approach was the best. Before going in he looked around, up and down the block, across the street, up at the balconies, galleries and rooftops.

"Are you lookin' for your friend?" she asked.

"Yes."

"See him?"

"No."

"Is he trying to play some kind of trick on you?"

"I wouldn't be surprised," he answered. "Okay, come on."

They went inside.

"Look at all this stuff," she said. "Isola would love it here."

"She probably did," he agreed.

"You mean she was here?"

"I think so. At least, the guy I talked to said he might have recognized her from my description."

"And you think they sent those two men after you from here?"

"Maybe."

"That's what you said about the Papa Legba."

"Yes," he said, "it is."

THIRTY-SEVEN

The same man—Malik—was sitting behind the counter.

"Ah, mon," he said, raising his hands, "I see you found her."

"No," Sangster said, "this is her sister."

"Eh?" Malik narrowed his eyes and studied Octavia. "Ah, yes, me can see dat now, mon. This one is younger, no?"

"Yes," Sangster said.

"So you saw my sister?" Octavia asked.

"I am sure of it now," Malik said. "Yes, she looked just like you. The same . . . uh . . . eyes."

"Have you seen her since I was here last?" Sangster asked.

"No, on, she ain't been here since den," Malik said.

"How about this?" Sangster took the grig-gris bag out of his pocket and put it on the counter. Malik shrank back from it.

"What de hell, mon?"

"Do you recognize it?"

"It's a gris-gris."

"From here?"

"Huh? Oh, I see. You mean did we sell it." Malik leaned forward, studied the bag for a moment. "No, mon, we don't carry dat one here."

"What about two men with Creole accents, one very thin, the other a big man?"

"Lots of men match dose descriptions, mon."

"Seen together?"

Malik shook his head. "I ain't never seen two men like dat together."

Sangster studied the man but he couldn't tell if he was telling the truth or not.

"Would you open this?" he asked Malik.

"You ain't opened it?"

"No."

"Well," Malik said, shaking his head, "me don't open no gris-gris, man."

"Why not?" Sangster asked. "Last time I was here I had the impression you didn't believe in Voodoo."

"That don't mean me push me luck, mon."

Sangster studied Malik again, then picked up the gris-gris and put it back in his pocket. "All right," he said.

"What about Sharise?" Malik asked, raising his eyebrows.

"Sharise . . ."

"Last time me tell you Sharise was a *Mambo* who work here," Malik reminded him.

Mentally, Sangster struck himself in the forehead with the flat of his hand. Of course! He was supposed to return here and talk to the woman. How could he have forgotten? It wouldn't have happened three or four years ago. Was he really a better man with a soul? Or just different?

"Is she here today?"

Malik nodded. "In the back."

Sangster looked at Octavia, who shrugged.

"All right, then," Sangster said. "I'll talk with Sharise."

"Dat be twenty dollar," Malik said, putting his hand out.

"What?"

"Twenty dollar for a sitting with de *Mambo*," the black man said, wiggling his fingers.

Sangster took out a twenty dollar bill and placed it in the center of Malik's palm.

"And for de girl?" Malik asked.

"We only need one sitting," Sangster said.

"Den de girl stay wit' me, mon."

Sangster stared at Malik, and the smirk on the man's face fade.

"Well," Malik said, "I guess dere's no harm in de girl goin' wit' ya."

"Thank you, Malik."

THIRTY-EIGHT

They had to pass through a beaded curtain to enter the back room, where Sharise apparently held court. The room was small, lit by candles, Voodoo paraphernalia adorned the walls. In one corner stood an altar, with candles and a metal bowl

In the center of all this, at a small round table, sat an older black woman with chalky skin and white hair tied atop her head. She could have been sixty or eighty.

Sangster almost expected to see a crystal ball on the table in front of her, or tarot cards, and Octavia said beneath her breath, "Oh, boy."

"Non-believer," Sharise said.

"What's that?" Sangster asked.

"You are non-believers," the old woman repeated. "You, at least, have some respect." She pointed a crooked, long-nailed finger at Octavia and added amid the sound of clanking bracelets, "She don't."

"Well," Sangster said, "it really doesn't matter if we're believers or not, we paid our twenty dollars."

"Sit, den," she said, with a disdainful wave of her hand.

Sangster took the seat. Octavia remained a couple of paces behind him.

"No crystal ball?" Sangster said, for no particular reason than to break the silence.

"Me ain't no mystic!" the woman snapped. "Whatchoo want?"

Instead of answering, Sangster dropped the gris-gris on the table top.

"What dat?" the woman asked.

"It's a gris-gris bag."

She expelled air from between her lips rudely and said, "Me know dat, fool! Whatchoo wan' I ta do wit' it?"

"Tell me what it means."

She prodded it with the same crooked finger, then looked at Sangster suspiciously.

"Where you get it?"

"In my kitchen," he said. "Two Creole men left it in my house."

"Where de doll?"

"There was no doll."

Now she made a "tsk" sound. "Dis ain't not'in'."

"What do you mean, nothing?"

"Dere ain't no doll," she said. "Real gris-gris connected to a doll."

"Is that so?"

"Yeah, dat so." She grabbed the bag, opened it and dumped out the contents. Despite himself Sangster shrank back. Enough people had already refused to open it. She dumped it out like a bag of French fries.

She poked at the contents with her long nail. Sangster thought he saw some hair—from his comb?—a swatch of cloth probably taken from an article of his clothing, what looked like fingernails (he didn't recall having clipped them that week), and a few other things he didn't recognize.

"Gris-Gris mostly used to make babies," Sharise said.

"What?"

"It used to make barren girl fertile," she said. "You wan' have a baby?"

"Uh, no."

"Den dis not'in." She raised both hands, bracelets clinking on both wrists, as if she had touched it enough. "You put de stuff back."

Hesitantly, he swept the content off the table and back into the bag.

"So," he said, putting the bag back in his pocket, "if I believed in Voodoo, this bag couldn't hurt me that way?"

She made the "tsk" sound again and said, "No, mon."

"Would they bring it with them?" he asked. "And then leave it?"

She leaned forward and said, "Mon, somebody tryin' ta scare you. You scare easy?"

Sangster was about to answer when Octavia said, "He ain't scared of nothin'!"

Sharise looked past Sangster at Octavia, narrowing her eyes, which were hazel, and remarkably bright.

"You, little girl," she said, "Me know you?"

"You don't know me."

"I seen you—" Sharise started, pointing again, but then she stopped. "No, me wrong. Me not see you, but somebody look like you."

"My sister!"

Sharise stared at her, then nodded and said "Yes, me see her. Her believe, not like you."

"When was she here?" Sangster asked.

"Last week, sometime," Sharise said, with a shrug.

"And what did she want?" Sangster asked.

"Why you look for her?" Sharise asked. "She missin'?"

"Yes," Octavia said, "she is."

Sharise sniffed and said, "Maybe she wanna be missin'. You ever t'ink of dat?"

"She was with another girl who was later found dead in Jackson Square."

Sharise's eyes widened. "Me hear dat? But dat girl strangled."

"So?"

"Stranglin', dat don't go wit' Voodoo."

"Isola's interested in Voodoo," Sangster said. "Like you said, she's a believer. But whether it's from Voodoo or not, she could be in danger."

"An' you wan' save her?"

"That's right."

"Why?" Sharise asked. "You her daddy?"

"Just a friend," Sangster said, and then added, "of her mother."

"Well," Sharise said, "dat girl interested in spells, and gris-gris."

"What kind?"

"All kind."

"How many are there?"

"Dere be four kinds of gris-gris," Sharise said, and ticked them off on her fingers, "love, power, luck, and uncrossing."

"What's 'uncrossing'?"

She "asked" again. "You crossed when you on a negative path, or you jinxed. Den you got to be uncrossed."

"I see." Sangster said. "Do you have any idea where Isola—the girl—went from here?"

"Me t'ink she went on a bad path," Sharise said. "A bad path."

"Okay," Sangster said, "thanks."

He turned to leave, but as Octavia went through the beaded curtain he turned back, thinking about Burke.

"Do you know how to undo spells?"

"Of course!"

"Do you make house calls?"

THIRTY-NINE

Sangster entered the hospital with Octavia and Sharise. The Voodoo *Mambo* had insisted she did not need to change her clothes to go out. "It only a dress." It was a loud, flowered dress, with the matching kerchief in her hair. She was a large woman, so she attracted a lot of attention as they walked through the halls.

As they went up the elevator she seemed nervous.

"Me don't like elevators," she said.

When they reached Burke's floor he led the way down the hall to the room. The ex-Sheriff was lying right where Sangster had left him. A nurse came running down the hall after them from the nurse's station.

"No change?" Sangster asked.

"None," she said. "Sir, you can't all go in there—"

Sangster looked around.

"Where's the cop on the door?"

"There hasn't been one all morning," she said. "I just assumed—"

"All right," he said, "never mind." It had been a few days. Telemaco probably couldn't justify the expense any longer. Besides, he had other cases, and was keeping an eye on the Grimes murder.

"We're not all going in," he told the nurse. "Just her."

"Her?" the nurse asked, looking at Sharise.

"And why not?" Sharise asked.

"Visiting hours aren't over," Sangster pointed out.

"Well, no—"

"Okay then," he said. To Sharise: "Go ahead. We'll wait out here."

Sharise nodded and went inside.

"Is she a doctor?"

"No, she isn't."

The nurse seemed to want to say something else, then just shook her head and walked back to her station.

"You gonna see your girlfriend while we're here?" Octavia asked.

"Girlfriend?" Sangster said. "What are you talking about?"

"The nurse in the emergency room," she said. "The red-haired one with the freckles."

"The emergency room nurse?" he repeated. "What makes you think she's my girlfriend?"

"Well," she said, indicating herself, "you don't like dark girls, right?"

"Octavia . . . you really should wear a bra."

"Now you sound like Father Patrick." She pouted. "You got change."

"For what?"

"The vending machine."

He took out whatever change he had in his pocket and handed it over.

"You want a soda?"

"No."

"I'll be right back."

"Don't leave the building, and don't talk to any strange men!" he called after her.

She waved without looking back.

Sangster remained outside the room for as long as Sharise was inside. He kept an eye up and down the hall for Quinlan. The man was going to have to reappear sometime. But instead of Quinlan showing up, he saw Polly coming towards him.

"Stark! Is somet'ing wrong?"

"No," he said, "I just came to see how he is." She looked around.

"You got 'Tavia wit' you?"

"Yes," he said, "she went to get something from a vending machine."

Polly looked into the room, took one step as if to enter, and then drew back suddenly.

"Why you got a *Mambo* in dere wit' him?"

"How do you know she's a *Mambo*?" he asked.

"I know it," she said, "and I know dat woman."

"Sharise?"

"Ha!" Polly said. "Dat de name she give you? Her name Bernice DeBois."

"And how do you know her?"

"Dat don't matter," Polly said. "I know . . . she a phony."

"Why would you call her a Mambo if you think she's a phony?" he asked. "Polly, are there some things you haven't been telling me?"

At that moment Sharise came out, stopping short when she saw Polly.

"Whatchoo doin' here?" she asked.

Polly didn't answer. She pushed past the woman and went into the room.

"What she doin' here?"

"You know Polly?"

"Polly? Dat what she call herself. Huh. Her name Portia when I know her."

"And where was that?"

"Back in Jamaica. We grow up together."

"I see."

"Whatchoo need me to see your friend when you got her?"

"What do you mean?"

Sharise laughed. "You don't know?"

"Don't know what?"

The heavyset woman let out a short laugh like a bark and said, "Whatchoo need me when you already got a *Mambo*."

She started off down the hall. Sangster saw Octavia standing there with her mouth open, and wondered how much she had heard, but he didn't have time to ask. He hurried after Sharise.

FORTY

Sharise couldn't talk in the elevator. She was too nervous, so they waited until they were outside.

"Sharise," he asked, "what you said in there—"

"About Portia?" she said. "Back in Jamaica she a *Mambo*. Not no more here, though, huh?"

"No, not here," he said, "but . . . that was a long time ago, wasn't it?"

"Well, yes," Sharise said. "She and me, we was—what do you call it--learnin'—"

"Apprentices?"

"Dat's it," she said, snapping her fingers. "We was apprentice to de same *Mambo,* but Portia, she don't like it none."

"And you?"

"Me like it fine," she said, with a grin that showed gold teeth.

"All right, so what did you see in that room up there?"

"Dat man, him in trouble," Sharise said. "Him gon' need help."

"From you?"

"No, not me, mon."

"Can't you do a—what do you call it—healing spell?"

"Healing spells are for small t'ing, wounds or sickness. Dis mon, him need a cure spell. The right potion."

"And you can't do that?"

She shook her head. "Me don't have dose ingredients."

"Do you know who would?"

She looked him in the eye and asked, "You believe now?"

"Let's just say I'm willing to try anything, at this point."

"Den maybe me can help you after all . . ."

Sangster took the elevator back up to Burke's floor, found Octavia in front of his room, staring through the doorway. When he reached her he saw Polly seated at Burke's side.

"Was that true?" she asked. "What she said? My mama is a *Mambo*?"

"No."

"But she said—"

"She said in Jamaica she and your mother were apprentices, but your mother didn't stick with it. She didn't believe in it."

"But she never even told us that."

"Maybe she will, some day," Sangster said. "That'll be up to her, won't it?"

"I guess."

He noticed her hands were empty.

"Didn't you find a vending machine?"

"It was broken."

"Come on," he said, "let's go to the cafeteria. We can get something there."

"Okay."

"Polly?" Sangster called.

She turned her head and looked at him.

"Are you hungry? We're going to the cafeteria. We can bring something back for you."

"No," she said, looking at Burke. "I'll come wit' you."

She took a last look at Burke, then stood up and joined them in the hall.

"Where'd she go?" she asked.

"She left."

"She's a fake."

"If you say so," he answered. "You'd know better than I would."

"Mama—"

"Later, 'Tavia," she said. "I will tell you everyt'in' . . . later."

"Yes, Mama."

They got to the cafeteria, grabbed a tray each and moved through the line. Sangster was surprised to find etouffe on the menu in a hospital. He decided to chance it.

Once their trays were filled, they walked to a table and sat down, the two women across from him. They had each gotten what looked like bowls of gumbo.

"Oh, God," Octavia said, after one taste, "it's awful."

"It is hot," Polly said. "Go ahead and eat it."

Sangster tasted the etouffe. To him it seemed all right. Polly and Octavia continued to eat their soup.

"Can I get another bowl?" Octavia asked, when she was done.

"Sure," Sangster said, giving her some money. "Go ahead."

The line was longer now, so it would take her some time.

"Polly," Sangster said, "I need your advice."

"Mine?" she asked, surprised. "What I can tell you?"

"Sharise suggested I go and see a man on Bayou St.

John," he said. "Apparently he's a *Houngan*. She says he'll be able to help Burke."

"So now you believe?"

"Not necessarily," he said, "but like I told somebody else, I'm willing to try anything."

"What advice you need?"

"The bayou," he said, "from what I've heard it's pretty far, and pretty rough." Sangster's knowledge of the bayou was confined to what he'd read and seen on TV and movies.

"Not Bayou St. John," she said. "It the only one inside the city limits of New Orleans. It not so bad. Who she tell you to see?"

"A man called *Houngan* Henry. Is that a legitimate name?" he asked. "It sounds . . . well, kind of mundane."

"It could be real," she said. "In Voodoo you supposed to not supposed to call *Houngans* or *Mambos* by dey first names, not wit'out their title."

"So Sharise would be *Mambo* Sharise?"

"Hmph!" Polly huffed and let her spoon drop into her empty bowl.

"Do you know someone who can take me to Bayou St. John?" he asked.

"I know someone," she said.

Octavia returned to the table with her second bowl of terrible gumbo and dug in. They stopped talking about Bayou St. John, started talking about Burke.

"He'll come around," Octavia said.

"What makes you so sure?" Sangster asked.

"Mama always says Burke is a tough old buzzard."

"Dat right," Polly said, with a smile. "Dat what I say."

"And you're right," Sangster agreed. "He is a tough old buzzard."

FORTY-ONE

Sharise had also told him something else at the hospital.

"The girl, the one you are lookin' for," she said. "It is her daughter?" She put great emphasis on the word "her."

"Portia's?"

"Yes."

"And that other girl?"

"Also her daughter."

"Pretty girls," Sharise said.

"Yes."

"And young."

"Very."

She fixed him with a steady look. "Bayou St. John."

"You told me that, Sharise."

"No, I mean dat girl," she said. "She say somet'in' about goin' to Bayou St. John."

"Anything else?"

"No," she said, "dat all I can tell you. Except . . . good luck."

"Sharise," he said as she started to walk away.

"Yeah?"

"The gris-gris bag," he said. "Did it come from Marie Laveau's?"

"No."

"Do you want a ride back," he called after her.

She just waved a hand without looking back . . .

* * *

Outside of Burke's room Sangster said to Polly, "I may have a line on Isola."

"Whatchoo mean, 'a line'?"

"I mean I may have an idea where she is," he explained. "I'm going to check it out. I want to leave Octavia here."

"You leave her," she said. "She always safe wit' me, but you bring my odder girl home, you hear?"

"I'll bring her home," he said, "and I'll find the sonofabitch who put Burke in here."

"You do dat," Polly said. "We see you at de church later."

"Did you leave Hugo with Father Patrick?"

She nodded.

"If you need a ride you call Father Patrick," he said. "The church has a car."

She nodded again.

"But before I leave, tell me who can take me to see Houngan Henry."

FORTY-TWO

Sangster peered down at the end of the dock, where a sad looking boat sat on the calm waters of Lake Pontchartrain. As he approached he saw a similarly sad looking black man sitting on the dock next to the boat, working intently on something in his hands that commanded all of his attention.

However, as Sangster came closer he could virtually see the man's ears perk up, and he stopped walking.

"You kin come ahead, friend," the man said, "an' tell me where y'at, you?"

"Are you Lew Allemand?"

The man looked up at him and said, "Dat me."

Sangster could see the man was doing delicate work, tying flies, and doing it remarkably well for a man with thick, sausage-like fingers. The black man's forearms were powerful, etched with ropey, bunched muscles. He knew from Polly that the man was in his seventies, but he could have easily passed for much younger. His skin was smooth and creamy, and not as chalky as that of some older Creole men.

"Polly Bourque sent me."

His hands still working the man said, "Polly good people. You good people, you?"

"I haven't always been." Sangster admitted, "but I'm trying."

The man stopped what he was doing, set the fly he was working on down, and stared up at Sangster with renewed interest.

"Dat a very honest answer," Allemand said.

"I figured the truth would serve me well."

"And so it should," Allemand agreed. "You a friend of Polly, then I can help you. What you want?"

"I want you to take me to St. John's Bayou."

"Dat across de river."

"I know," Sangster said.

"Why you wanna go dere?"

"I'm looking for a man."

"What man?"

"His name's Henry."

A grave look came over Allemand. "You mean Houngan Henry?"

"That's right."

"Dat a bad idea, brah," the black man said. "Real bad. You take my word for it. Dat part of St. John's Bayou still kinda wild. Like back in Marie Laveau's day."

"I've got to go out there and see him. And since you obviously know who he is, you can not only take me there, you can introduce me."

"Oh no, not me, brah," Allemand said. "Dat man, he scare me."

"Well," Sangster said, "then just take me over and point the way so I don't get lost."

"Brah, you know what used to go on out dere?" Allemand asked. "You do know de stories of Auntie Laveau, don't you?"

"I've heard them."

"Dat's where she done all her voodoo rituals," Allemand said. "Dere's souls still out dere, brah. I don' wan' be runnin' into dem souls, me."

"That was then, Mr. Allemand," Sangster said. "This is now. What do you say?"

"Den you are bound and determine' to go?" the black man asked.

"Yes, sir."

"And you'll pay?"

"I'll pay."

"Then do not call me Mister, and not sir," Allemand said. "Call me Lewis."

"All right, Lewis. When can we leave?"

"And your name?"

"Stark."

"Mr. Stark—"

"Just Stark."

"—it's goin' be dark soon. You don' wan' be on Bayou St. John when it's dark." Lewis shook his head. "I wouldn't want to be out dere, me."

"I want to be there as soon as possible. Let's just settle on a price."

"Is it just you," Lewis asked, "or will dere be your friend, too?"

"What friend?"

"Dat fella at the end of the dock," Lewis said, jerking his chin. "Is he your friend?"

Sangster turned and saw the man Lewis was referring to. He was tall, standing stock still, watching them. When he saw Sangster looking at him, he still didn't move. From that distance his face was hidden from sight, but Sangster knew who he was.

"That's no friend of mine," he told Lewis. "It'll just be me. When can you be ready?"

"You heard of a fella bein' born ready, brah?" Lewis asked. "Dat be me."

"Then give me a minute," Sangster said. "I'll be right back."

"And I be ready," Lewis said. "Me and my boat.

FORTY-THREE

When Sangster reached Quinlan he stopped about three feet away. The man looked at him and smiled.

"Takin' a little boat ride?" he asked.

"What's it to you?" Sangster asked.

"I wouldn't want you to drown," the hitman said. "That boat don't look too sturdy."

"It's not the boat that might kill me as much as what's out on the bayou," Sangster said.

"Gators?"

"Among other things."

"Like?"

"The souls of the dead, they tell me."

"Ah, souls," Quinlan said. "I don't believe in them, myself. Men like you and me, we start believin' in souls and they'd start to haunt us. Be pretty tough for us to keep doin' our jobs, then. Oh, but wait. You don't do it anymore, do you?"

"No, I don't."

"I wonder . . ."

"About what?"

"How you could stop," Quinlan said. "I mean, cold turkey, just like that."

"It's not something you'd understand."

Quinlan sighed. "You're probably right."

Quinlan looked past him at Lewis Allemand and the boat.

"So, when do you think you'll be back?"

"Before morning, I hope. Why don't you just wait here for me?"

"Naw," Quinlan said. "I don't like bein' near the water very much. I think I'll go back to the hospital, look after the ladies for you."

"What?"

"You know," Quinlan said, "that pretty little girl and her mother."

"Quinlan," Sangster said, "if you hurt them—"

"And why would I do that," Quinlan asked, cutting him off. "I got nothin' against them. Besides, what do you have to threaten me with? You don't kill anymore, remember? Well, except for Vegas last year, right?"

"I don't murder anymore," Sangster said. "I don't kill for profit. That doesn't mean I'm ready to just roll over."

"Okay, then. I don't want you to have to be worryin' about the ladies when your mind should be on other things. A man could get killed like that. No, I'll just make sure they get home safe."

Sangster studied the man and decided that he was telling the truth. And he thought he knew why.

"I want your mind to be real clear," Quinlan said, "when I come for you."

Yep. That was why.

Suddenly, Quinlan reached behind him and came out with a Glock in his hand. It was pointed at Sangster's belly until the man reversed it in his hands and held it out to him.

"You might need this."

"I don't think so."

"You never know," Quinlan said, "what with the gators and such. I mean, you are goin' into a swamp, right?"

Sangster stared at the gun.

"I know you don't like the more modern weapons," Quinlan commented, "but I don't have any Webley's on me." Mentioning Sangster's favorite gun showed that the man had done his research.

"That's fine," Sangster said, taking the Glock. "This will do."

For just a moment he thought that he could solve the problem of Quinlan just by pulling the trigger. If the gun was in good firing order.

He worked the slide, examined the weapon briefly.

"Oh, it works," Quinlan assured him. "You could put a bullet in me right now easy as pie."

Sangster tucked the gun into his belt.

"That's where you're wrong," Sangster said. "For me, it wouldn't be that easy."

He turned his back and walked the length of the dock back to Lewis and his boat.

FORTY-FOUR

"You are not a policeman, are you?" Lewis asked when they were on the lake.

"Huh?" Sangster had been deep in thought. The sound of the boat's engine was soothing to him. Quinlan had been right. It didn't look like a very sturdy vessel, but it seemed to run all right.

"A cop," Lewis said, "*gendarme?*"

"Oh, uh, no, I'm not a cop."

"I t'ink maybe your friend should have come wit' you," Lewis said. "I would not want to be going out to Bayou St. John alone, me."

"I told you, he's not my friend," Sangster said. "Besides, I'm not alone. I've got you."

"I takin' you only so far, brah," Lewis warned him, "and den you on your own."

"Deal," Sangster said.

Lewis nodded, then turned his attention back to the direction the boat was heading.

And Sangster went back to his thoughts . . .

He'd been thinking about guns.

After what had happened in Vegas he had discarded the two Webley's he'd bought there. He'd killed people with them, and didn't want to keep them around. But when he decided to go to Bayou St. John he considered taking Burke's .45 with him, however he decided against it. But when Quinlan offered him the Glock, and he took it, the gun felt so right in his hand.

He put his hand on it now, leaving it in his belt. It was a comforting presence. It wasn't a betrayal of his soul to think that way, was it?

He'd been thinking about his soul a lot more lately—even more than usual, especially after meeting Father Patrick. He was wondering how much he should tell Father Patrick about his past. Maybe, if he told him all of it, the priest could help him figure this soul stuff out. Or maybe he'd be appalled. If Sangster was Catholic, he could have broached the subject in confession, but there was no way he could convert just for that.

Maybe if he and Patrick became friends it would change things. After all, the man didn't really strike him as an ordinary priest. He'd come to the vocation late in life, and he didn't really seem to be toeing the party line. Maybe he'd apply the same attitude to Sangster's past.

It was getting darker by the minute.

"How much further?" he asked Lewis.

"Not far," Lewis said, "but you still got to go a little ways by canoe."

"Canoe?"

Lewis nodded.

"It called a pirogue. Got a flat bottom. Only way to get deep into the bayou."

"Deep?" Sangster asked.

Lewis looked back over his shoulder and said, "Deep."

"Great . . ."

He thought about what he and Quinlan had said about souls. He himself insinuated that the bayou—St. John's Bayou—was filled with the souls of the dead, left over from the days of Marie Laveau. Quinlan said if men like them started believing in souls they'd be out of a job. Well, that's what happened. Sangster discovered his soul and quit. But did the presence of a soul mean he had to change completely? After all, cops and soldiers had souls and they killed people when they had to. Maybe what he had done in Vegas—killing men who were basically gangsters, if that word even still applied these days—didn't put too much black on his soul. That was certainly a question Father Patrick should be able to answer for him, at some point.

But what if souls were these ethereal things that actually were still trapped on Bayou St. John after what Marie Laveau had done to them many years ago?

"Hey, Lewis."

"Yeah, brah?"

Sangster stood up and joined Lewis at the wheel.

"Do you believe in souls?"

"You askin' a Creole man who lives in New Orleans if he believe in souls?"

"Do you believe in the souls of the dead?"

Lewis looked at him.

"You startin' to have second thoughts about goin' to Bayou St. John, brah?"

"Lewis," Sangster said, "I start my days off with second thoughts. I'm having third and fourth thoughts about this."

It was dark by the time Lewis pulled his boat in at a rundown dock.

"You sure about this?" Sangster asked. "There aren't even any buildings here."

"There's a canoe," Lewis said, pointing.

"So we switch now to the canoe?"

"Dis where you switch to the canoe."

"Me?"

"You da one wants ta see Houngan Henry." Lewis pointed. "You take da canoe down dat tributary, all de way to de end."

"Alone?"

"Alone. You ain't scared, are you?"

Back when he didn't know anything about souls he would have said no. He couldn't remember ever being scared when he was on a job. But now . . .

"Scared shitless, Lewis."

"Dat's good," Lewis said, "'cause dere ain't no *fais do do* waitin' for you at de udder end."

Lewis walked with Sangster to the canoe, held it steady while he got in. Then he handed him an oar.

"You ever been in a canoe before?"

"Once or twice."

"You jus' keep changin' sides with de oar," Lewis said, "you gets where ya goin'."

"I got it, Lewis."

"Well, dere ya go," Lewis said. "*Laissez les bon temps roulez.*"

"What's that mean?"

"Dat French for 'let the good times roll'."

FORTY-FIVE

It was dark. The only light Sangster had to maneuver by was the moon. The part that was hidden to make it appear oblong, but it gave off a lot of light.

Sangster had more than second thoughts about being out in the bayou this late at night, but there was nothing he could do about it now. He was committed. And he probably should have been.

The only steady sound was his oar working in the water. There were other sounds—birds, fish, maybe even a gator or two if he cared to look. Once something big brushed up against the side of the canoe. He didn't look, preferring to believe it was a big tree branch floating in the water. Had he seen that it was an alligator, he might have panicked. That was something else he had never done while on a job. Maybe having a soul wasn't such a great thing after all, if it made you frightened and panicky.

He thanked God for the light of the moon, then realized that might have been the very first time in his life he ever thanked God for anything.

The swamp started to spread out around him, but as Lewis had instructed, he maintained a straight course. He kept his jacket on, even though it was still oppressively hot this late at night. But if he removed it he knew he'd be eaten alive by insects that seemed to be increasing the further he went. Besides, when he got out of the canoe the jacket would hide the gun, and gris-gris in his pocket.

Suddenly, up ahead he thought he saw a light. He stopped his oar work for a moment to just stare ahead, narrowing his eyes. The light was gone, but then was there once again. Finally, it seemed to remain lit and he started rowing again. It had to be where he was headed—and, if not, maybe somebody could put him back on the right track.

Lost in the Louisiana bayou late at night . . . this definitely was not the smartest thing he had ever done. Not by a longshot.

Scared . . . hell yeah, he was scared.

The light remained constant, as he was got closer. But every time he thought he was almost there, he saw that he was wrong. So he just kept going, thankful for the light up ahead for giving him a goal, even if it turned out to be the wrong one.

Suddenly he was almost there, causing him to work his oar a little faster—left, right, left, right—until he saw a small dock and, beyond it, a shack with a lighted window. Obviously, this was the light he'd been rowing toward. As his canoe drifted to a stop against the dock he slapped a fat mosquito on his neck, his palm coming away red with blood.

He hoped it wasn't an omen.

FORTY-SIX

Sangster stood carefully and stepped onto the dock, pleased that he'd managed to do it without falling into the water, thankful for the pirogue's flat bottom. He'd once fulfilled a contract while on a yacht, and got seasick while doing it. Thankfully he'd avoided that condition this time.

Before heading for the shack, he zipped his jacket to cover the gun. Something thrashed about it the water and he unzipped it again in case he had to reach for it. Having a soul certainly didn't preclude him from shooting a gator if he had to.

He started for the shack slowly, keeping his eyes on the light in the window. As he approached he couldn't see any shadows inside. It was eerily quiet now, with not even the sounds of his oars in the water to break it up. He looked around, not knowing what he expected to see. If there were souls of the dead out here, what would they look like? Or feel like?

The front door was plain and pitted, and rather flimsy. He stopped in front of it and knocked.

"Come!" a man's voice called from inside.

He opened the creaking door, which swung outward, and stepped inside. The only light in the room was the one he had been staring at for the past hour or so. It was a storm lamp that sat on a rickety looking wooden table.

A black man sat at the table and looked up at Sangster. He had one startling grey eye and the other was milky white. He was very thin, almost emaciated, and obviously well advanced in age. He had only a white fringe of hair around a shiny bald head. There was something leather in his hand. Various objects were scattered on the table. Drawing on his very limited experience, Sangster realized the man was fashioning a gris-gris bag.

"Whatchoo want?" he asked. He had an amazingly hearty, bass voice for a man who was so frail looking. "Who you be?"

"My name is Sangster." He was surprised he had given the man his true name—or, at least, a name that was more truly his than "Stark" was. "I'm looking for someone."

"You lookin' in de wrong place, brah," the man said.

"I hope not," Sangster said. "I came a long way to talk to you—that is, if you're Houngan Henry."

The man stared at Sangster intently for a few moments with that one grey eye.

"I be Henry. How you get here?"

"I, uh, came in a canoe."

"Alone?"

"Yes, sir."

"Don't call me sir," the man said. "You call me by my title."

"Yes . . . Houngan."

Houngan Henry pointed with an oddly graceful gesture and said, "Pull dat chair over here."

Sangster turned, saw a sturdy, handmade wooden chair, grabbed it and pulled it over to him.

"Well," Henry said, "sit!"

Sangster sat.

"What's wrong wit' you, boy?"

"Actually," Sangster said, "I don't know. I just feel kind of . . . strange."

"It be de soul."

"What?"

"Soul," Henry said again.

"You mean . . . the souls of the dead?"

"Soul," Henry said, pointing again. "I mean maybe . . . it be your soul."

Sangster's eyes were adjusting to the semi-darkness of the interior of the shack. Behind Houngan Henry, in a darkened corner, was what looked like an altar.

"What do you mean by that?"

"Your soul," Henry said, "it is new to you . . . no . . . foreign."

"Yes," Sangster said.

"So you have come here to learn about it?"

"No, that's not it," Sangster said. "I'm here looking for a girl named Isola Bourque."

Houngan Henry did not react to the name at all. Sangster was suddenly concerned that this trip might not have been necessary. Had Sharise sent him here for her own reasons?

As if reading his mind, Houngan Henry asked, "Who sent you to me?"

"A woman named Sharise," Sangster said. "Oh, sorry, Mambo Sharise."

"*Mambo?*" Henry asked. "Is that what she callin' herself?"

"Isn't she a *Mambo?*"

"Take a lot more than the name to make someone a priestess of Vodun." Another word for Voodoo.

"So you do know her?"

"I know her," Henry said, "but I do not know why she would send you to me. We are not . . ."

". . . friends?"

"Exactly."

Sangster frowned. "She wanted to get me out here for some reason."

"Only two I can think of for a man to come out here," Henry said.

"What are they?"

"Like me, if you live here," Henry said. "Or . . ."

At that moment they both heard something bump into the side of the shack.

". . . to die here," Sangster finished.

FORTY-SEVEN

Sangster got up from his chair and moved to the window. It was grimy, but he could see outside. The moon was still high and bright, but he didn't see anyone.

"I'm going to have to go out there," he said.

"Why?"

He turned to look at Henry, who shrugged his bony shoulders.

"Somebody's out there," Sangster said, "probably here for me. In fact, there may be more than one."

"Two, t'ree," Henry said, "maybe more."

"Exactly."

"Then stay here."

"I don't want to put you in danger."

The old man laughed, that deep bass rumbling around in his concave chest.

"I am in no danger," he said. "No one would dare come in here without my permission."

"You mean," Sangster said, "if they believe in Voodoo."

"A believer would never approach me."

"But what if there are some non-beliers out there?" Sangster asked.

The old Voodoo priest considered the question.

"I still say wait," he said, then. "Make them come in after you."

"No," Sangster said, "it's too dangerous."

"It is dangerous out there," Henry said.

"Maybe," Sangster said, touching the gun in his belt,

"or maybe one of them will get grabbed by a gator."

"I was not talkin' about gators, cher," Houngan Henry told him.

Sangster stared at the old man for long moment, realizing that he was referring to something more otherworldly than an alligator. Then his attention was drawn outside again when something brushed the side of the shack.

They were trying to draw him out.

He drew the Glock from his belt, turned toward the door.

"Stay away from the bank on de left," Houngan Henry said.

"Why?"

"Dat where my friend Papa Legba stay."

"Papa Legba?" Sangster asked. "*The* Papa Legba?"

Henry smiled, showing some gaps in his teeth.

"No, cher, dis Papa Legba a big ol' gator. Him been shot many times, but him still out here, and him like dat left bank. It belong to him. Understand?"

"I understand."

"And, cher?" Henry said.

"Yes?"

"If you must kill tonight," the Houngan said, "your soul will survive it, you."

Sangster adjusted his grip on the Glock and asked, "Are you sure?"

Henry nodded, then said, "When this is over, we will talk."

"I'd like that," Sangster said.

FORTY-EIGHT

Sangster stepped outside with the Glock in his hand. The door was centered so he had to look both ways. Now that he was doing something his body was very familiar with, he felt an odd calm come over him. Or maybe it was what Houngan Henry had told him about his soul. Either way, his heart was beating evenly, his breathing under control and he was only sweating from the cloying heat of the bayou.

But he had a feeling he was dealing with people who knew what they were doing. If not they might have come in after him, trapping themselves in a small, confined space. Or maybe he was giving them too much credit and they had stayed out from respect for Houngan Henry.

Sangster had no choice but to pick a direction. His canoe was off to his right, and the gator, Papa Legba, was off to the left. He started to go right when he heard something from that direction, so he quickly darted left, and around the corner, alert in case they had herded him that way. No one was on that side of the building, though, so he flattened himself against the wall and peered back around to the front. A black man, slick with sweat, came from the other side of the building, moving slowly. As he moved along the front he made sure to rub his hip against the wall, and even knocked a few times, making the sound Sangster had heard while inside.

Sangster looked behind him again. He was expecting someone to come from the rear of the building. If there were more than two, he could ill afford to miss this chance of taking out one of them—but he preferred to do it without killing him.

He listened intently, wondering if the man was going to stop at the door. He didn't. He kept going right past it, still rubbing up against the building. Perhaps there was another man, or more, doing the same thing on the other side.

All he had to do was wait for the man to reach him, hopefully before another one appeared. He heard a sound from the banks of the bayou, assumed it was Papa Legba thrashing around. As long as the gator stayed on his side they'd get along fine.

He heard the man getting closer, and then saw his arm appear. As he came around the corner, he saw Sangster. His eyes went wide and he opened his mouth to yell, but Sangster was too fast for him. He smashed the guy in the face with his gun, knocking him cold, caught him and lowered him to the ground. He looked around for someplace to hide him. There was a stand of cypress trees behind him, so he dragged him there and stowed him out of sight. Before leaving, he searched him and came up with a gun, a small, flat automatic. At least the man wasn't carrying a Voodoo doll or gris-gris bag. A gun Sangster could handle. He snatched it from the man's belt and tossed it into the brush.

One down, but how many to go?

Behind the house were two more black men. One was Claude, who had been in Sangster's house. The other was Lloyd, the even bigger man Sangster had met at the Papa Legba Gallery.

"I don't hear Marcel," Claude said.

"Dat boy a fool," Lloyd said. "You go fat way, I go dis. You see dat *souris* you shoot him dead, you hear?"

"I hear," Claude said, thinking it was funny that Lloyd referred to the man as a mouse. "But let's hurry. Me don't like it out here. The Widow Paris, dey say she still out here."

"Marie Laveau longtime dead, brah," Lloyd said. "You keep your mind on what you doin'. Now go!"

They were standing against the rear wall of the shack. Lloyd pushed Claude off to his left, and he went right. They each had a gun in their hand.

Sangster decided he needed some distance from the shack. If the other man or men were still trying to scare, they were probably working in opposite directions. They'd be coming around the house the way the first man had.

Instead of moving away from the cypress tree where he hid the first man, he joined him in there.

Off to his left he heard splashing and realized he was now closer to the gator's left bank. He just hoped this Papa Legba had a better temperament than the original one.

Inside the house Houngan Henry lit the candles on his altar and knelt in front. He burned something in a small, metal tray, and fanned the smoke that came up from it.

"Papa Legba," he said, "hear me . . ."

Outside the man at Sangster's feet started to come to, so he hit him again. He hoped this time he would stay out until it was all over.

He slapped at a fat mosquito on his neck with his left hand, held the gun in his right, and kept his eyes fixed on the shack.

FORTY-NINE

In the old days he would have just taken them out, fired from where he was and be done with it. As his life stood now, he'd never be able to justify it to himself as self-defense. It didn't matter that there were no cops in the bayou, or that the bodies could be easily disposed of by just feeding them to Papa Legba—either one.

Did he long for the old days, then?

No.

He was going to have to try to take them off balance and disarm them, and then . . . what?

He looked around at the banks of the bayou, but saw only his own boat. How had they gotten out here? If he disarmed them and left in his pirogue—then what? They must have had a way out. They might even beat him back to New Orleans, and be waiting for him there.

He wondered if Houngan Henry would hold the men here and give him a good head start?

But before he did anything he wanted to know who sent them. Who were these men working for? Were they working for Kate from the Papa Legba Gallery? Or, since it was Sharise who had sent him out here, were the men working for her?

Or were they all working for someone else he was not even aware of yet?

But first things first. He needed to get the drop on them.

The cypress trees he was hiding in were about thirty feet from the house. He could close most of that distance before they heard him coming. All he had to do was wait for them to show . . .

Lloyd stopped.

He had almost come around to Sangster's side of the house when he heard something. Pressing his ear to the thin walls of the shack he listened. From inside he could hear a droning sound—a voice. He recognized it. The voice of a Houngan, chanting.

This was not good.

Claude didn't hear the droning. He just kept moving along the wall of the house, grinning and scraping a branch he'd found, against the side of the house. This would surely frighten the men inside.

He moved along the front of the house, past the front door, stopping at the corner, where he expected to see Lloyd—but did not.

He stopped, feeling confused.

Sangster saw the man stop and look around. Obviously, he'd expected to meet someone there. So where was the other man? Then he saw him, and recognized Lloyd, who was moving slowly along the side of the shack, until he reached the other man. They put their heads together. If he broke from cover now they'd see him too soon, resulting in a definite shootout.

So he waited.

"He's chanting," Lloyd said.
"Who?" Claude asked.
"Who you t'ink? Houngan Henry."

"He jus' an old man."

"He a Houngan!"

Claude made a "tsk" sound with his mouth.

"Why don't we just go in and get dat guy?" he asked.

"Dat maybe what we have ta do," Lloyd said.

"Good," Claude said, and headed for the door. Lloyd hesitated, then followed.

As soon as they turned their backs to head for the front door, Sangster broke his cover and started to run the thirty feet between them. He had to stop them before they could enter the shack and maybe end up shooting Houngan Henry.

He was moving quickly, sure he was going to make it when Lloyd suddenly looked over his shoulder. His eyes widened, he started to turn, and yelled to the other man.

"Don't do it!" Sangster shouted, holding the Glock out in front of him.

The other man turned as Lloyd shouted, and was quicker with his gun. He brought it to bear on Sangster, who had no choice but to fire. He pulled the trigger once.

The man with the gun shouted again—this time in pain—and threw his hands up. The gun went flying away from him as he fell onto his back.

Lloyd still had to draw his gun from his belt. He was in the act when Sangster pointed the Glock at him.

"Please don't," he said to the big Creole man.

Lloyd frowned, hesitated, then his face was split by a big grin. He took his hand away from his gun.

"You do not wish to shoot me," he said.

"No, I don't."

"Excellent!"

"Drop the gun."

"Of course."

"Use two fingers!" Sangster barked.

Lloyd's fingers were like sausage links, but he managed to take the gun from his belt daintily and drop it to the ground.

"Now," he said, "I am unarmed."

"That's right."

Lloyd lowered his hand and took a step toward Sangster.

"Stop there."

"Or what?" Lloyd asked. "You will shoot me wit' dat gun? I do not think so."

Sangster knew he was right. He couldn't kill the man while he was unarmed.

Lloyd grinned and stepped forward with more confidence.

"Lloyd . . ." Sangster said, warningly. "You know I can't let you get those big hands on me."

"Den you better shoot," Lloyd said, "or run."

Sangster heard Papa Legba, the gator, thrashing around on the bank, and said to Lloyd, "Well, I sure as hell don't want to run."

He pulled the trigger.

FIFTY

Sangster got a rag from Houngan Henry and gave it to Lloyd to wrap around his injured foot. He had put a bullet right through the man's instep, figuring—and rightly so—that would stop him in his tracks.

Lloyd wrapped the foot as well as he could, all the while cursing Sangster in Creole French.

"What's he saying?" he asked Henry.

"Better you do not know," the old man said.

"Yeah, you're probably right."

Lloyd was sitting on the ground with his back to the wall of the house. Houngan Henry had come out when the shooting stopped, seemed pleased to see Sangster on his feet. It was the first time Sangster had seen the man on his feet. He was very short—even though, for his age, he stood very straight.

"I had to kill one of them," Sangster said, sadly.

"Do not worry, cher," Henry said.

After Lloyd had his foot wrapped, he quieted down a bit, except for an occasional moan.

"How'd you get here?" Sangster asked.

"In a boat," Lloyd said. "It is further down." He pointed to the right, away from Papa Legba's bank.

"Did you get here first, or follow me?" Sangster asked. He would have sworn up and down that he hadn't been followed.

"We were ahead of you, brah," Lloyd bragged. "We have been ahead of you from the start."

"And who is we?" Sangster asked. "Who are you working for?"

"Dat I can't tell you, brah," Lloyd said, shaking his big bald head.

"Was there another man?" Houngan Henry asked.

"Yes," Sangster said. "I left him in the trees." He jerked his chin to indicate the stand of cypress trees behind him.

"Those trees?" Henry asked, pointing. "Dat's a bad place to be, brah. Better you get him out. Maybe he talks to you."

"Yeah," Sangster said, "maybe he—"

He was cut off by the sound of a man screaming. A big, fat gator came out of the brush, dragging the screaming man by the leg, crawling to his left bank.

"I tol' you," Houngan Henry said. "Bad place."

Sangster swallowed, realizing he had spent quite a bit of time in those cypress trees.

"Well, Lloyd," he said to the big man, "that leaves you."

Lloyd was still watching the writhing man being dragged by the gator, and he turned his wide eyes toward Sangster.

"Or would you like to discuss it with Papa Legba, there?" Sangster asked.

FIFTY-ONE

Sangster had one of his disposable cell phones with him. Unfortunately, there was no signal in the bayou. He wanted to head right back to New Orleans, but Houngan Henry convinced him to wait until morning.

"You were lucky to get here," the old man told him. "It will be safer to go back in daylight."

"I'm worried that my boat pilot won't be there to take me back," Sangster said.

"Was it Lewis Allemand?"

"Yes, that's him."

"Do not worry," Henry said. "He will be there."

They got Lloyd inside the shack to keep Papa Legba from getting him, and then they all tried to get some sleep. Lloyd slept fitfully, and his moaning made it hard for Sangster to get more than a few winks.

Sangster saw Houngan Henry sitting at his table and joined him there.

"You cannot sleep, you?" Henry asked.

"Our friend's moaning is keeping me awake."

Henry got up, went to a wood burning stove, poured something into a mug and brought it back to Sangster.

"Here?"

"What is it?" Sangster asked. "Some Voodoo potion?"

"Yes," Henry said, "it is called tea."

Sangster tasted it. It was, indeed, tea, and tasted so good.

Henry sat down again, across from Sangster.

"I feel you did not finish what you wanted to say

earlier, you," the old man said. "I have not seen this girl you are lookin' for."

"I have another problem," Sangster said. "I have a friend in the hospital, in a kind of coma that the doctors can't treat, because they don't know what's caused it."

"And you think it was caused by Voodoo?"

Sangster didn't answer right away, then said, "I'm just about ready to try anything, at this point."

"What do you want of me?"

"Can you come to the hospital and look at him?"

"Have you brought anything of his with you?"

"No."

"I have not left dis bayou for a very long time, me."

"Houngan—"

"I will have to consider your request," Henry said. "Finish your tea and try to sleep. You should leave at first light."

Sangster nodded. He'd done what he could here. It was time to go back.

They heard something moving out in front of the shack, and when they came out the next morning they realized that, during the night, the gator had come for Claude's body.

Sangster got Lloyd into his pirogue, because the boat the big man had used with his partners had managed to drift away. So Lloyd was all that was left of that landing party.

Rowing back through the bayou in daylight was not as harrowing an experience as it had been during the night, but neither was it a walk in the park. In the daylight he could see the gators and water moccasins.

When they reached Lake Ponchartrain, Sangster saw Lewis and his boat waiting at the little dock.

"I wasn't sure you'd still be here," Sangster said.

"I wasn't about ta leave you in da bayou, brah," Lewis said. "Who your friend?"

"Not so much a friend," Sangster said, "but I need help to load him onto your boat."

Between them they got the big man onto Lewis' boat, and then Sangster tied off the pirogue so it would be there for the next person.

"Did you see Houngan Henry?" Lewis asked.

"I did."

"He give you what you want?"

"Not really," Sangster said, "but there's still hope."

"We betta get back, den."

Sangster untied Lewis' boat from the dock and pushed off.

Lloyd remained silent for the entire ride. Sangster kept trying his cell phone, but there was no signal and he assumed there wouldn't be until they actually reached New Orleans.

All the way back he thought about Polly and Octavia, wondered if they had gotten back to the church and Father Patrick safely. Having Quinlan's Glock with him had probably saved his life, but he still didn't feel comfortable leaving their safety in the hitman's hands.

When they reached the dock Sangster tied the boat off, then tried his cell phone. He got a signal, and dialed Telemaco.

"It's Stark."

"Where y'at, Stark?" the detective asked.

"Can you meet me at the hospital?" he asked the detective. "I've got something for you."

"A bag of beignets?" Telemaco asked.

"No," Sangster said, "but bring some with you, will ya?"

"Yeah, sure. This got something to do with Burke?"

"And the girls."

"I'll see you there."

"The emergency room," Sangster said, just before the man hung up.

He broke the connection and looked at Lewis. The boatman helped him get Lloyd up onto the dock, where the big man teetered on one leg.

"Thanks again for waiting, Lewis," Sangster said.

"Did you doubt?"

"I did, for a minute," Sangster admitted, "but Houngan Henry assured me you'd be there. I don't understand how he knew."

"He should know," Lewis said. "He my brudda."

He got back into his boat before Sangster could say anything else.

"Let's go, gimpy," he said to Lloyd.

"I gotta lean on you, brah."

"Yeah, well," Sangster said, "if you try anything I'll put a bullet in your gut. Got it?"

"I got it."

They limped to the end of the dock where Sangster was surprised to find Quinlan waiting.

"Here you go," he said, handing the man his Glock.

"Did it come in handy?" Quinlan asked.

"It did. Thanks. You get those girls home last night?"

"Took them to church," Quinlan said.

"Great," Sangster said, "now if you help me get this big piece of shit to my car . . ."

"Let's go," Quinlan said, getting on Lloyd's other side and putting his arm around his shoulders.

Sangster still couldn't figure the man out.

FIFTY-TWO

Sangster drove Lloyd to the hospital. Telemaco was waiting at the emergency room entrance with two uniformed cops.

"Who's this guy?" the detective asked.

"My gift to you," Sangster said. "Help me get him inside, and then I'll fill you in."

They hauled Lloyd out of the car and he hissed when he got to his feet.

"What happened to him?" Telemaco asked as they walked the big man into the hospital.

"Somebody shot him in the foot."

"Should I even ask who?"

"No."

Inside the emergency room they were met by Claire O'Malley.

"Well, hello," she said to Sangster. "What have we here?"

Sangster looked at Telemaco.

"A man with a gunshot wound to the foot," the cop said.

She looked around, grabbed a wheelchair and pulled it over.

"I'll take him."

They sat Lloyd down in it. She grabbed the handles, looked at Sangster, said, "Don't go away," and wheeled the injured man off.

"Go with them," Telemaco told the cops. "Don't let him out of your sight."

"Right," one of them said.

"Okay, Stark," Telemaco said, turning to Sangster, "give."

There was a bag in Telemaco's hand.

"Beignets?"

"Yep."

"Let's go find some coffee."

When they were settled at a table in the cafeteria with two coffees, they opened the bag of beignets. Sangster found he was starving.

While they ate Sangster told Telemaco about going out to Bayou St. John and how he spent the night. He told him about the three men who had attacked him and Houngan Henry, and how he recognized one of them from his house.

"The one who told ya'll he knew where the girl was?"

"Yes."

"And this guy? Had ya'll seen him before?"

"Yes, when I went to the Papa Legba Gallery, looking for Isola."

"Okay," Telemaco said, "so you think these three men are involved in the girl disappearing. And maybe my dead girl?"

"I do."

"So where are the other two?"

This was his first real lie on the subject.

"A gator got them."

Well, not really a lie.

"A gator?"

"A big one."

"And who shot this other fella foot?"

Now an out-and-out lie.

"He did it himself," Sangster said. "When the gator came at them, he panicked and pulled the trigger."

Telemaco eyed Sangster suspiciously.

"It sounds like a gator came along real conveniently to save your bacon."

"That's not just what it sounds like," Sangster said. "It happened."

"And the old man ya'll went to see? He's a witness to everything?"

"He is."

"And he'll testify, if necessary?"

Sangster hesitated, then said, "I don't know about that. He says he hasn't left the bayou in years."

"Maybe," Telemaco said, "we should deal with first things first. I'll see what this fella with the shot foot can tell us about the girls."

"And don't forget," Sangster said, "he works at the Papa Legba Gallery, and that's where you'll find Sharise, who sent me out to the bayou in the first place." Then something occurred to him. "Wait a minute. I'm getting mixed up."

"It's no surprise," Telemaco said. "When did ya'll last sleep?"

"I can't even remember."

"What's the mix up."

"Lloyd—the guy with the shot foot—works at the Papa Legba. Sharise works at Marie Laveau's House of Voodoo."

"Well," Telemaco said, "it's all the same to me. I'll check both places. What are you going to do?"

"Me?"

"You've obviously been running your own investigation."

"I've just been looking for my friend's daughter," Sangster said. "If you can find her, I'll be happy to butt out."

"Just lookin' for your friend's daughter, huh?"

"That's right."

"And you ended up with a target on your back—twice—because of that?"

"I must've been getting in somebody's way."

"Ya think?" Telemaco asked. "Uh-oh, heads up." He looked past Sangster, to where his partner had just entered the cafeteria. "He don't like you a lot."

"I'm not too fond of him, either," Sangster said.

"Just sit on that feeling for a couple of minutes, will you?"

"You got it."

"Those two uniforms told me I'd find you here," Williams said. He gave Sangster a sour look, then brightened when he saw the bag. "Any beignets left?"

"Plenty," Telemaco said.

"Okay, I'll get a coffee and then you can fill me in."

He cast another look of distaste at Sangster as he left.

"Ya'll should leave now, before he comes back," Telemaco said. "I'll call you when I know something, or when I need you."

"Okay."

"Ya'll got anything other than a land line?" Telemaco asked. "A cell phone number?"

"No cell phone," Sangster said.

"Everybody carries a cell phone," Telemaco said.

"Not me," Sangster said. "I don't want anybody calling me when I'm out. Phone calls are for home and phone booths."

"A bit of a dinosaur, aren't you?"

"Pretty much."

"Well, you right about that. I feel pretty much the same way. Here comes Williams. You better get."

"See you," Sangster said, and got.

Sangster went back down to the emergency room just to make sure Lloyd hadn't made a break for it. He wasn't looking for Nurse O'Malley, but she found him.

"Where'd you go?" she demanded.

"Oh, I had to talk to the police."

"Are you all right?" she asked. "You look all warn out. What'd you do, spend the night in the bayou?"

"As a matter of fact, I did."

"Oh!" She was surprised into silence for a moment. "Well, I thought maybe I'd hear from you after, uh, the other night, but I guess you've been busy."

"Um, oh yeah, I, uh, I have been," he said. "I'm, uh, sorry."

She smiled then. "You're very cute when you're flustered, you know that?" She touched his face. "Call me when you can."

"I will," he said. "I promise."

"No, don't promise," she said. "Just do it." She slapped his cheek lightly, then pulled her hand away. "That way there are no broken promises."

"Okay," he said. "Claire."

"Ah, very good," she said. "You remembered." Then she heard something over the P.A. system and said, "I've got to go!"

For a brief moment Sangster wondered if he should risk getting involved with a woman, again. Then he put the question aside for another time.

He spotted Telemaco and Williams coming back into the emergency room, and got out of there.

FIFTY-THREE

Sangster went directly to Algiers to St. Mary's and knocked on the door of the Rectory. Mrs. Cox answered, saw the look on his face and said, "Don't worry, Mr. Stark. They're all here."

"Thank you, Mrs. Cox."

She led him into the living room area, where Polly was sitting reading, Hugo was watching a small color TV, with Octavia staring at the screen, obviously not interested. However, when she saw Sangster she sprang to her feet.

"Dude," she said, "are you all right? What happened to you?"

"Did you see him?" Polly asked.

"I saw him."

"Who?" Octavia asked. "Who did you see?"

"Will he help?" Polly asked.

"I don't know."

"Who are we talkin' about?" Octavia asked.

"Never mind, 'Tavia," Polly said. "Mr. Stark look like he need a shower and some sleep."

"You got that right," Sangster said. "I just wanted to make sure you both got here safe last night."

"That guy you told me not to talk to came and got us," Octavia said. "He swore you sent him, and Ma believed him."

"I did send him," Sangster said.

"But you told me not to ever talk to him again. Are you friends now?"

"No," Sangster said, "last night was an exception to the rule."

"So I shouldn't talk to him if I see him again?"

"Hopefully, you won't be seeing him ever."

"And what about Isola?" Polly asked.

"I gave Detective Telemaco some information that might help locate her," Sangster said. "We'll find out something in the morning." He looked at Mrs. Cox. "Is Father Patrick in the church?"

"He is," she said. "He had some paperwork to do in the Sacristy."

"Thanks," he said. "I'll see you ladies—and you, Hugo—tomorrow."

The boy waved without taking his eyes from the TV screen.

"I'll come with you," Octavia said.

"No," Sangster said, "I want to talk to Father Patrick alone."

"'Tavia, stay here," Polly said. "Let Mr. Stark do what he got to do."

"Oh, all right." The young girl folded her arms and dropped back into her chair. "This blows."

Sangster couldn't have agreed more.

As Sangster entered the church from the rear he saw that Patrick wasn't in the Sacristy, but up at the altar. What seemed off to Sangster was that the priest was just staring up at the crucifix.

Sangster had never understood a religion that worshipped a man nailed to a cross. But then he'd never understood any religion. And even with a soul, he was still stumped by them—Jewish, Catholic, or Voodoo.

As he walked down the aisle, Father Patrick turned to watch him. The priest didn't say anything until the ex-hired killer reached him. Sangster noticed that Patrick was clutching a Bible so tightly his knuckles were white.

"You caught me," he said.

"Caught you doing what?" Sangster asked.

Patrick hesitated a moment, then said, "Questioning."

"What were you questioning, Patrick?"

Father Patrick stared at Sangster for a few moments before answering.

"I'm going to tell you the truth, Stark," he said. Then, "Even though I don't feel you've told me the truth. Not all of it, anyway. But I think you and I are kindred spirits." He paused, and Sangster let him have the moment. "I was questioning my faith—well, not my faith, but whether I'm doing the right thing. I believe in God, but I'm not sure I believe in the Church, or in what I'm doing here. Have you ever done that? Questioned what you chose to do with your life?"

Sangster studied Patrick for a moment, decided that the man actually was opening up to him and telling the truth.

"More than you know, Patrick," he said. "And you're right. I haven't told you the whole truth."

"Well, I wish you would, Stark," Patrick said, "if that's even your name. I wish you'd open up to me, not as a priest, but just as a friend."

Patrick came down from the altar and stood level with Sangster.

"You know, Patrick," Sangster said, "when this is all over, I may just do that."

"I look forward to it, my friend," the priest said. "Hearing your story might actually help me write the next chapter of mine."

"I hope both of our next chapters end well," Sangster said. "Can we sit down a minute?"

"Sure."

Patrick sat in the first pew, Sangster the second. He

explained everything to Patrick that he'd told Polly and Octavia.

"You do look like you've been through the wringer, my friend," Patrick said. "And you stink."

"I know," Sangster said, "I'm going home to take a shower, but I'm coming back."

"We have a shower here," Patrick said, "and I can loan you some clothes."

"No, that's okay," Sangster said. "There's something else I have to pick up. I won't be gone long, and then I'd like to spend the night."

"What makes you think that's necessary?"

"Two things," Sangster said. "Now that I've turned Lloyd over to the police, somebody might come after me again at my house."

"So you'd also be safer here, like Polly and her kids?"

"Well . . . maybe."

"What's that mean?"

"I'm thinking somebody might also be coming here," Sangster said, "and I'd like to be here just in case."

"You think these Voodoo people will send someone after Polly and Octavia?"

"I'm not really thinking about Voodoo, Patrick," Sangster said, "but something a little more tangible."

"But—"

Sangster stood up.

"I'll be back in under an hour."

The man across the street, hidden in the dark, watched as Sangster left the church, got into his car and drove away. He was sure the man would be back soon, so he had to act fast.

He crossed the street and entered the church through the door that Father Patrick had failed to lock behind Sangster.

* * *

Father Patrick was walking up the center aisle to lock the door when it opened and a man stepped in.

"I'm sorry, sir," he said. "You might not understand it, but we do lock the door to God's house."

"I'm sorry, Father," Quinlan said, pointing his gun at Patrick, "but I'm going to need you to do exactly what I tell you."

Patrick froze and stared at the gun. He had not seen Quinlan the night before when the hired killer brought Polly and Octavia home.

"Sir, are you sure you want to do this?" he asked. "Are you sure you're even in the right place."

"Oh, Father," Quinlan said, "I'm in the right place."

FIFTY-FOUR

Sangster took a shower, dressed in clean clothes, then left his house and crossed over to Burke's. He went inside, stayed only minutes, then came out and got into his car. He drove directly to the Rectory and was knocking on the door in less than an hour, as he had promised.

When Mrs. Cox answered he knew from the look on her face that something was wrong.

"Mrs. Cox?"

"Oh, Mr. Stark," she said, "they're in the church—they're all in the church."

"All?" he asked.

Sangster ran to the church, found the door still unlocked. He entered and saw them all in the front—all but Quinlan, seated in the first pew. He was standing there, legs spread, hands clasped in front of him, just waiting.

"Hey, Sangster," he said. "Welcome to church, man."

"Quinlan," Sangster said from the back, "what's this about?"

"Well, I think you know. Why don't you come closer and join us? And spread your arms for me."

Sangster was wearing a black T-shirt and jeans, no jacket this time.

He walked down the aisle toward Quinlan, with Father Patrick, Polly, Octavia and Hugo watching over their shoulders from the first pew.

"Okay, stop there," Quinlan said, when Sangster had about twenty feet to go to reach him. "That's far enough." He raised his right hand, which was holding the Glock.

"Why don't you let them go, Quinlan?" Sangster asked. "This is between you and me."

"I'll let them go in due time."

"What's going on?" Sangster asked. "Why would you help me, and then pull this?"

"Head games, man," Quinlan said, "or mind games. Whatever you want to call them, that's my thing."

"Well then, it's working," Sangster said. "I'm confused."

"I've got a rep," Quinlan said, "but you still have a bigger rep, even though you've been out of the business for a few years."

"What business is he talking about, Stark?" Octavia asked. "And why does he call you Sangster?"

"Hush, girl!" Polly said.

"No, it's all right," Quinlan said. "Let the girl talk. She's got questions for the man she should ask them while he's still around to answer."

"Still around?" Octavia asked.

"You gonna kill Mr. Stark?" Polly asked.

"That's the plan."

"You just gonna shoot him in cold blood?" Father Patrick asked. "Without giving him a chance?"

Quinlan thought a moment and then said, "Father, you obviously don't know who we're dealing with here. This is the kind of man you don't really want to give much of a chance to."

All of the people in the front pew turned their eyes to Sangster, who remained quiet.

"And on that note," Quinlan said, "put your hands in the air, Sangster, and do a slow turnaround for me, will you?"

Sangster obeyed, raising his hands and turning slowly.

"That's what I thought. Take that piece from the back of your belt and drop it on the floor. And use two fingers to do it. You know the drill."

Sangster reached behind him, briefly considering if he could draw the old .45 Peacemaker quick enough to out gun Quinlan, even though the man was already pointing the Glock at him. He decided against the move, plucked the gun from his belt with two fingers, holding it out in front of him, and then dropping it to the floor.

"Jesus," Quinlan said, "how old is that piece? I know you like old guns but . . . does it even fire?"

"Why don't you let me pick it up and we'll find out?"

"Naw, naw," Quinlan said, then seemed to think about it and added, "Well, maybe. We'll see."

"How long is this going to take, Quinlan?" Sangster asked. "I'm really tired."

"I don't blame you, after spending all night out on the bayou like you did. I'm surprised a gator didn't get you."

"I only made it back thanks to your Glock," Sangster pointed out.

"Well, I'm glad I was able to help out."

"You helped him," Father Patrick asked, "just so you could kill him?"

"Professional courtesy, Father," Quinlan said.

"Professional—" Father Patrick said, then stopped. "I don't think I understand."

"I think maybe you do, Father," Quinlan said, "and maybe you don't like it. Maybe your friend, here, ain't what you thought he was."

"I don't judge my friends," Patrick said.

"As for your question, Sangster," Quinlan said, "this ain't gonna take long at all. In fact, just to make sure, why don't you kick that old hogleg over here."

Sangster looked at Father Patrick and knew the priest was going to try something. There was no way he could stop him.

Patrick put his left hand on Hugo's chest, shielding the boy with his body, as he stood and threw the thick Bible he was holding at Quinlan.

The heavy book opened as it flew through the air, which slowed its progress, but it still had enough force to startle Quinlan when it struck him in the shoulder. He turned quickly to his left before he realized his mistake.

Sangster moved the second Quinlan's head moved. He dove for the Peacemaker on the floor in front of him. Quinlan turned back, saw Sangster on the floor and tried to bring the Glock to bear on him. Sangster's hand closed over the Peacemaker and he brought it up. He fired a split second before Quinlan squeezed the trigger. The bullet from the ancient gun hit Quinlan in the center of the chest, driving the air right out of him. The Glock went off, followed by the sound of broken glass. Somewhere in the church a stained glass window had taken the worst of it.

Father Patrick was holding Hugo close to him, while Polly was doing the same for Octavia.

Sangster got to his feet and walked to the fallen killer. The Glock was lying alongside him, so Sangster kicked it away. He looked down at Quinlan, saw that the man's eyes were fluttering. He crouched down.

"It didn't have to be this way, Quinlan."

Quinlan's eyes were glazed, but he managed to fix them on Sangster. He laughed shortly, spitting blood from his mouth.

"Let myself be taken by a retiree," he gasped, "with an ancient cannon."

He died.

Sangster stood and looked at the others.

"Everybody all right?"

"Yes," Patrick said, "we're fine, but Sangster . . ."

"Yeah?"

". . . you're shot."

Sangster looked down, saw the blood on his chest. The bullet had gone through him before breaking the glass.

"Shit," he said.

Father Patrick rushed to catch him before he could hit the floor.

FIFTY-FIVE

When Sangster woke the first thing he saw was white. He realized he was staring up at a white ceiling. He closed his eyes and listened to the sounds around him, realized he was in a hospital. He felt like he'd been run over by a truck, but he was alive—for now.

He opened his eyes again, squinting against the light and the white. Turning his head helped a little. He saw the machine he was hooked up to, which was making a beeping noise. And he saw the nurse.

"There you are," Claire said.

"Wha—" he started, but his mouth was too dry to speak. She took a cup from the table next to him and held it to his mouth so he could drink with the aid of a straw. It was water, and it did the trick.

"What are you doing here?" he asked.

"I'm a nurse."

"An emergency room nurse."

"Well," she said, "I had a vested interest in your condition."

"And what is my condition?"

"It was serious," she said. "Now that you're awake it may be upgraded."

He tried to look down at himself, saw that he was swathed in bandages.

"How bad?" he asked.

"The bullet went in your chest and right through. The doctors are amazed it missed your heart, and didn't hit anything else vital. Just a lot of tissue damage and blood loss."

"I'm a lucky man."

"Yes, you are."

"How long have I been here?"

"Two days."

"And you . . ."

"No," she said, "not the whole two days." She took the water cup away and set it down. "I'm not that invested. I'll get the doctor—oh, and the police want to talk to you."

"Priest . . ." he said, going dry again.

"You want a priest?" Then she got it. "Oh, your friend the priest."

He nodded.

"Yes, he's outside. I don't think anyone would object if I sent him in."

She left the room. Moments later Father Patrick entered.

"Stark," he said, "or should I call you Sangster?"

"Stark would be best for now," Sangster sad. "Water, please."

Patrick held the cup for him, and he drank his fill, this time.

"Are Polly and her kids okay?" he asked.

"They are," Patrick said. "And I mean all of them."

"They found Isola?"

Patrick nodded. "Detective Telemaco did. I'm sure he'll fill in all the details for you. He didn't tell me any more than that." Patrick looked over his shoulder. "He should be here soon."

"You probably shouldn't be here when he is."

"Right," Father Patrick said, "you wouldn't want me talking about anything I heard."

"Patrick," Sangster said, for the man was not wearing his collar, "we can talk about what you heard later."

"In private."

"Right."

Patrick nodded. "Okay. I think we both have things to talk about, after you've recovered."

Patrick backed away from the bed, then stopped.

"I'd offer you my blessing," he said, "but it wouldn't be worth much after today."

Sangster didn't find out what that meant until later.

FIFTY-SIX

Nurse O'Malley came back with the doctor, an older man with white hair and pink skin. He examined Sangster's wound, both front and back, then applied a fresh dressing.

"The edges of the entry and exit wounds are clean," he said. "You should heal nicely."

"Thanks, Doc."

"Thank Father Patrick," the doctor said. "Rather than wait for an ambulance he threw you in his car and got you here."

"I will thank him."

"There's a police detective in the hall wanting to see you."

"You can send him in," Sangster said. "I feel stronger."

"Good."

"When can I go home?"

"Not for a while," the doctor said, "and when you do, you'll need some home care."

"Maybe you'll recommend someone," Sangster said.

"I will," Claire said, giving Sangster a look.

"I'll send the detective in," the doctor said.

"Thanks again, Doc."

The man nodded and left. Sangster ran his right hand over the bandages, which had been wrapped him tightly, binding his left arm to his chest so he couldn't move it.

Detective Telemaco came in, smiling. Nurse O'Malley nodded to him, said, "I'll be right outside," to Sangster, and left the room.

"Sangster, where y'at," Telemaco said. "I thought you were done. When I got here they were working on you in the emergency room. There was a helluva lot of blood. Guess you were lucky."

"Maybe," Sangster said. "Can't say the same for the other fella. That cannon put a mighty big hole in him. I'm glad it fired. I had my doubts."

"Well, it did the job."

"Talk about doing the job," Sangster said, "I heard you found Isola."

"And the other two girls, thanks to you," Telemaco said. "Your pal Lloyd and his cousin Sharise were running a scheme that people at the Papa Legba Gallery and Marie Laveau's had no idea of."

"A scheme?"

"Drugs," Telemaco said.

"And the girls?"

"They were pokin' around, saw somethin' they shouldn't've."

"And the dead girl?"

"Lloyd said that was an accident," Telemaco said. "Apparently he doesn't know his own strength. He says the girl's neck just broke."

"I thought she was strangled."

"Well yeah, but the hyoid bone in her neck snapped," Telemaco said. "Even if she lived she wouldn't ever have been able to speak again. Funny, but that's the only damn bone in the neck."

"Yeah," Sangster said, "funny. And what about Burke?"

"He was pokin' around, and they had to get rid of him," Telemaco said. "Lloyd was waitin' for him in Pirates Alley and lowered the boom on him. He thought he'd killed him."

"Sloppy."

"Yeah, well, murder wasn't big Lloyd's first choice of

profession. He thought he'd killed Burke, and killed the Grimes girl by accident."

"What were they going to do with the other girls?" Sangster asked.

"They didn't know. They were holdin' them until they could figure it out."

"And this was all Lloyd and Sharise?"

"To tell you the truth, I don't think so," Telemaco said. "I think they were workin' for somebody else. I can't believe the people at the Gallery and Marie Laveau's were that ignorant. Especially the Gallery. There was some hinky stuff goin' on up on their second floor."

Sangster remembered the charred marks he'd seen on the floor there.

"Where were they keepin' the girls?"

"They were movin' them around," Telemaco said. "We found them right there on the second floor of the Gallery. The woman there—Kate?—claims she didn't know anything about it, and I can't prove otherwise."

"My money's on her for the brains."

"Yeah, well, I'll be keepin' my eyes on her from now on."

Sangster shifted, trying to get more comfortable.

"I better let you rest or that nurse will have my hide."

"Am I in trouble for what happened in the church?"

"Not according to Father Patrick, Polly and the kids," Telemaco said. "Seems you didn't have much choice. You saved their lives."

"Give Father Patrick credit," Sangster said. "He threw that Bible."

"Yeah, well, we'll get a full statement from you when you're up to it."

Telemaco headed for the door.

"Hey, Detective."

"Yeah?"

"What about Burke?"

"Nobody told you?" Telemaco asked from the door.

"Told me what?"

"Your buddy Burke," the detective said, "he's awake."

EPILOGUE
One week later . . .

"You wanna mind your business?" Burke said to Patrick.

"Sorry," Patrick said. "It's just different when you're watchin', you know? You see things—"

"Well, keep 'em to yourself," Sangster said from the other side of the chess board, cutting him off.

"Okay, okay," Patrick said, raising his hands. "Geez."

"What are you boys arguin' about?" Claire asked, coming out of the house carrying a tray with a coffee pot and mugs.

"Nothing," Sangster said, "Patrick's just bein' a dick."

"Hey," she said, "that's no way to talk about a priest."

"Ex-priest," Patrick reminded her.

"I'm sorry," she said, "as a good Catholic girl I'm still hoping that's temporary."

"I'm afraid not," Patrick said. "That's not a decision I came to lightly."

"Of course not," she said. "I'm sorry." She put her hand on Sangster's right shoulder. The left side was still swathed in bandages. "Are you okay? You shouldn't be sitting up so long."

"I'm fine," he assured her.

"Then I'll leave you alone." She kissed him on the cheek and went back inside.

All three men watched her walk away. She was

wearing a T-shirt and tight jeans. They weren't used to seeing her out of her nurse's uniform.

"You're sure gettin' some good professional home care," Burke said. "Hope it ain't costin' you an arm and a leg."

"It's not costing me anything," Sangster said.

"Ah," Patrick said, "love is in the air?"

"I don't know," Sangster said, studying the board. "I don't know if I can afford to let her hang around."

Burke understood the danger, and Patrick thought he was starting to.

"Are you stayin' in Algiers after you heal?" Burke asked.

"I haven't decided that, either."

"Well, I hope you do," Burke said. "After all, what're the chances somebody'll come lookin' for you again?"

"I don't know," Sangster said. It had happened twice already, so what *were* the chances?

After ten minutes Burke said, "Checkmate," and sat back, looking weary. His pallor was bad.

"You better go get some rest, old man," Sangster said.

Burke put his hand to his still bandaged head and said, "I think you're right."

Burke stood up and Patrick quickly took his chair and began setting the pieces up for a game.

"You know what I still can't figure?" Burke said.

"What's that?" Sangster asked.

"How come I woke up right after the doctor said some old Creole man came to see me?"

"Damned if I know."

"You don't suppose there was some truth in that Voodoo stuff."

"Hey," Sangster said, "you were a lawman around here for a lot of years. You know more about Voodoo than I do."

"Never put much stock in it," Burke said.

"Speakin' of Voodoo," Patrick said, "how's Polly and her kids doin'?"

"Polly's just fine," Burke said. "Octavia's just as sassy as ever, but Isola, she's bein' kind of . . . quiet, these days."

"After what she went through, I'm not surprised," Sangster commented. "But maybe she and her mother will get along better now."

"I hope so," Burke said. "That woman works hard for her kids. That boy of hers is a champ, but them girls . . ." He shook his head.

"Octavia's not so bad," Sangster said.

Burke touched his head and said, "I'll see you fellas later."

"Sure thing," Patrick said, making his first move.

Burke looked at Sangster and tossed his thumb Patrick's way.

"Is he gonna be around here from now on?"

"I don't know who's going to be around here, Burke," Sangster said, "but if I'm not, you're gonna need somebody to play chess with."

"Hmm," Burke said, and headed over to his own house.

"He doesn't like me much, does he?" Patrick asked.

"Give him time."

Sangster made a move.

"So," Patrick asked, "Are you gonna stuck around after you heal?"

"I don't know," Sangster said, "are you gonna stick to your guns about leaving the church?"

Patrick scratched his head. "Maybe we still have some stuff to talk about."

Sangster shrugged and said, "Maybe we do."

AUTHOR'S NOTE

Certain liberties were taken with some depictions of New Orleans—like some of its streets, shops, and bayous. If anyone detects what they think are errors, please know that they were made for reasons.

ABOUT THE AUTHOR

Randisi is the author of the "Miles Jacoby," "Nick Delvecchio," "Gil & Claire Hunt," "Dennis McQueen," "Joe Keough," and "The Rat Pack," mystery series. THE HONKY TONK BIG HOSS BOOGIE, the first book in the Auggie Velez Nashville P.I. series, appeared in 2013. UPON MY SOUL is the first book in the "Hitman with a Soul" Trilogy. He is the editor of over 30 anthologies. All told he is the author of over 600 novels.

He is the founder of the Private Eye Writers of America, the creator of the Shamus Award, the co-founder of Mystery Scene Magazine.

MYSTERIES BY ROBERT J. RANDISI

<table>
<tr><td valign="top" width="50%">

The Miles Jacoby Series
Eye in the Ring
The Steinway Collection (aka
Beaten to a Pulp)
Full Contact
Separate Cases
Hard Look
Stand Up

The Nick Delvecchio Series
No Exit from Brooklyn
The Dead of Brooklyn
The End of Brooklyn

The Gil & Claire Hunt Series
Murder is the Deal of the Day
The Masks of Auntie Laveau
Same Time, Same Murder

The Joe Keough Series
Alone with the Dead
In the Shadow of the Arch
Blood on the Arch
East of the Arch
Arch Angels
Back to the Arch (forthcoming)

The Dennis McQueen Series
The Turner Journals
Cold-Blooded

</td><td valign="top" width="50%">

The Rat Pack Series
Everybody Kills Somebody
Sometime
Luck be a Lady, Don't Die
Hey You, with the Gun in Your
Hand
You're Nobody til Somebody
Kills You
I'm a Fool to Kill You
Fly Me to the Morgue
It was a Very Bad Year
You Make Me Feel So Dead
The Way You Die Tonight

*The Auggie Velez/Nashville
Series*
The Honky Tonk Big Hoss
Boogie
The Last Sweet Song of
Hammer Dylan
The Festival of Death (working
title)

Stand Alone Crime Novels
The Disappearance of Penny
The Ham Reporter
Curtains of Blood
The Offer
The Bottom of Every Bottle
The Picasso Flop

Collections
Delvecchio's Brooklyn
The Guilt Edge

</td></tr>
</table>

www.ingramcontent.com/pod-product-compliance
Lightning Source LLC
Chambersburg PA
CBHW061535210726
48287CB00006B/1965